Ryder
Nicola Jane

Ryder Copyright © 2019 Original title Capturing A Renegades Heart - Nicola Jane

Ryder Copyright © 2024 Updated version – Nicola Jane

All rights are reserved. No part of this book may be used or reproduced in any manner without written permission from the author, except in the case of brief quotations used in articles or reviews. For information, contact .

Disclaimer

This book is a work of fiction. The names, characters, places, and incidents are all products of the author's imagination and are not to be construed as real. Any similarities are entirely coincidental.

Cover Designer: Wingfield Designs

Spelling Note
Please note, this author resides in the United Kingdom and is using British English. Therefore, some words may be viewed as incorrect or spelled incorrectly, however, they are not.

Trigger Warning

This book contains triggers for violence, explicit scenes, and some dirty talking bikers. If any of this offends you, put your concerns in writing to Ryder, the club's President, and he'll get back to you . . . maybe.

Please Note
Ryder was originally published as 'Capturing A Renegades Heart' in 2019. It was taken off sale in 2022 and is now returning with a new cover and some slight changes to the story (although no major plots have been changed.)

Playlist

REACT – Ella Enderson ft Robert Miles
Cold Heart – Elton John ft. Due Lipa
Vampire – Olivia Rodrigo
positions – Ariana Grande
traitor – Olivia Rodrigo
Slow Hands – Niall Horan
Mr. Brightside – The Killers
Happier – Marshmello ft. Bastille
I ain't worried – OneRepublic
Shoop – Salt-N-Pepa
Push The Button - Sugababes
Easy On Me – Adele
Here With Me – d4vd
Scars To Your Beautiful – Alessia Cara

Contents

Chapter One	1
Chapter Two	8
Chapter Three	15
Chapter Four	24
Chapter Five	33
Chapter Six	40
Chapter Seven	47
Chapter Eight	54
Chapter Nine	64
Chapter Ten	73
Chapter Eleven	82
Chapter Twelve	91
Chapter Thirteen	101
Chapter Fourteen	112
Chapter Fifteen	124
Chapter Sixteen	135
Chapter Seventeen	146
Chapter Eighteen	156

Chapter Nineteen	165
Chapter Twenty	172
Chapter Twenty-One	180
1. Epilogue	186
Social Media	191
About the Author	192

Chapter One

Neve

I crouch in front of my miserable five-year-old daughter, wiping her chubby wet cheeks with the pads of my thumbs. "Come on sweetie, it really isn't so bad. You'll be back home before you know it and I'm sure your Daddy has so much planned that you won't even have time to miss me," I reassure her, even though it's killing me to push her, when she doesn't want to go.

She sniffles again, more tears rolling down her rosy cheeks. "He doesn't play with me, he's always too busy," she cries. I know she's right, she's not being dramatic. I doubt Finn wants to see Harlee anymore than she wants to see him. He never wanted her from the second I found out I was expecting, and nothing's changed, apart from now I've left him she's his key to get to me.

"How about when you get home tomorrow, we go out to the cinema, or we can just stay home and watch films all day? You get to choose." Harlee nods her head, her sad frown still marring her innocent face. I hate Saturdays, I hate handing my little girl over to my ex-husband, but I know he'll make my life hell if I don't.

The low sound of rumbling fills the air and I watch my new neighbour rolling his motorbike to a stop. The guy only moved in a week ago, and already he's driving me insane. His noisy bike has woken Harlee more than once during the night.

He dismounts the large machine and removes his helmet. As annoying as he is, I can't help but check him out at every opportunity. It isn't often you got to see a six-foot something biker on your doorstep looking as good as he does. His brown shoulder length hair is pulled back into a tight man bun and even though I never go for guys with long hair, I feel strangely attracted to the biker. Having a six pack, tattoos and a golden tan, helps his cause.

"Good morning Siren," he says with a wink. He pulls a rose from his side of the fence and saunters towards us. Bending down on one knee he holds out the rose to Harlee, who giggles and accepts it with a curtsy. "And good morning to you, Ms Harlee. Why do you look so upset?"

"I have to go and see my Daddy," she mutters, looking down sadly at the rose. Griffin stands, towering over me so I have to tip my head back to see him clearly.

"Well Siren, you kept that quiet, you're not with the little ones Daddy?" he asks, arching a brow.

"My name is Neve," I reply, indignantly, "And why would I tell you anything about my personal life." We have the sort of banter where I pretend he's not hot and he pretends I'm his world.

"Because we're neighbours. I'm old fashioned that way, and I like to be able to walk into each other's houses and borrow a cup of sugar, talk about our day and discuss relationships."

I watch the black car stop outside of my house. "You'd better not walk into my house uninvited, or I'll put a knife in your chest," I whisper to Griffin, as I take Harlee by the hand and step closer to the vehicle.

Max, Finn's driver, steps out from the driver's side. "Finnegan had better be in the back Max, I've already told him that he needs to be here to collect her," I warn. I've had countless arguments because Finn likes to send a car to collect his daughter rather than turn up himself. The last time it happened, I'd refused to let Max take her, resulting in a huge argument between us both.

"Relax Neve he's in the back," Max says, like he's bored of my nagging, while pulling the door open. Finn steps out, casting his eyes briefly towards Griffin, who remains watching the whole exchange with interest.

I take note of his expensive suit and his designer shoes and roll my eyes. Coming around this area dressed like that, is purely for attention. *Why can't he just wear what normal men wear at the weekend.*

I've never had the same interest in money as Finn, which was why I only take a small amount from him in maintenance money to help raise Harlee.

Finn steps towards me and places his hand on my lower back, dangerously close to my arse. He kisses the side of my head, and then picks Harlee up and kisses her on the cheek. "How are my girls?" he asks, smiling. I shudder, he makes my skin crawl with his smarmy ways.

"Harlee is feeling a little unsettled, please spend time with her Finn," I warn him firmly.

"I always do," he replies passing her to Max, so that he can secure her in her car seat. "What are your plans for the evening?"

I contemplate not telling him, but I know it'll end in an argument, and Harlee is already upset. "Mya is popping over for a catch up, and then I plan on an early night." Finn places his finger under my chin and raises my head so that I'm looking at him.

"I'll call you later. Answer." He places a firm kiss against my lips and gets back into the car.

"Let me kiss Harlee." Finn opens his door, indicating that I should lean over him to kiss her goodbye. I sigh and lean over his knee, noting that he places his hand over my arse for a second time. "Be a good girl and we'll watch whatever movies you choose tomorrow, okay." I place tiny kisses all over her face, making her giggle. "I love you Popple," I whisper.

"I love you too Mummy," she replies, looking slightly happier.

I watch the car drive away, my heart aching in my chest. "You have a kid with Finnegan Lawrence," says Griffin, stepping forward and giving me a quizzical look. It isn't unusual for people to recognise Finn, although those that do are usually criminals.

"Was he responsible for saving your arse, or putting it away?" I ask, turning back towards my house and heading up the path.

"I don't need bent lawyers to save me, I rely on the truth."

I glance back and give him a smile. "I have to get inside and tidy up. My friend is coming over. It was nice catching up, but remember what I said Griffin, stay out of my house unless I invite you."

He gives a salute and a cheeky wink, "Understood Siren."

I spend the next few hours cleaning the house from top to bottom to take my mind of Harlee. By the time Mya arrives, I'm shattered. I pour two glasses of Prosecco and pass one across the breakfast bar to Mya. "So, Finn rang to ask if Harlee's allergic to fish, because he tried to give her some, and Harlee told him she couldn't eat it. I mean how does he not know that she's allergic to it?" I ask angrily. "It's not like

I haven't drummed it into him. And you know what he said? That kids are too finicky these days and they must eat it to build a tolerance up. I almost had a fit I was so mad. I mean, why the hell does he think I put her epi-pen in her bag?" I groan, "I hate sending her to him."

"It's a good job you've taught Harlee well, and that she recognises what she can and can't have. Honestly, I don't know what you ever saw in the creep." Mya shudders for added effect.

"Excuse me, I believe it was you that said he was fit and that I should go over and talk to him!" I remind her.

"Well he looked like Alexander Skarsgård, I thought he'd be cute like Eric in True Blood, but then you got to know him and I realised he was more like Perry Wright from Big Little Lies, and suddenly, he was less attractive." I laugh again at her comparison between a Vampire and a psychotic wife beater. Unfortunately, the second was much more accurate. When I first saw Finn, I'd convinced myself it was love at first sight. I'd been out celebrating my twentieth birthday with friends and Mya had dragged me over to where Finn was sat in the VIP area of the night club. We'd hit it off instantly, and after that I'd been swept off my feet. I saw the constant calls and text messages as him showing his love because he was so genuine each time he asked where I was and if I was okay, or what time I'd be home.

My friends thought it was cute that he worried. Alarm bells didn't really ring until my wedding night. Finn had kept up a good act for almost a year. Once we married on my twenty-first birthday, he'd shown his true colours by forcing himself on me. Turned out that Finn liked to be fought off during sex. The fighting and the forceful sex happened a lot, and then I fell pregnant at twenty-two, which pissed Finn off.

He couldn't push me about while I was carrying his child, and so he looked elsewhere.

The marriage finally came to an end when Harlee was born. Finn decided that he no longer loved me and preferred the single life. I wasn't heartbroken; I was relieved. I'd been wanting to get away since the day I'd found out I was pregnant. I didn't want a child around our volatile relationship, but I knew I'd never be able to leave him through my own choice, because he wouldn't let me, everything must be on his terms. When he announced his decision, I played the heart broken wife, but inside I'd been so God damn relieved.

"Earth to Neve," Mya says, waving her hand in front of my face. "I said, what the hell is all that noise?"

I hear the rumblings of motorcycles and sigh, "That Mya, is my new neighbour and his friends." Mya dives up from her seat and races to the window in the living room. She carefully parts the blinds so she could peek outside. I told Mya all about the sexy biker next door after he moved in, and she'd practically begged me to introduce them, to which I refused. She might be tired of being single, but I refuse to set her up with a biker.

"Let me take the rubbish out or something," whispers Mya.

"Are you serious?" I laugh, shaking my head.

"Yes," hisses Mya, "Get me the rubbish bag, quickly, I need an excuse for a closer look." I smirk as Mya ties her T-Shirt up over her navel to show off her flat stomach. She tousles her shoulder length blond hair and wipes her fingers underneath her eyes to remove any stray eyeliner. I hand her the waste-bag and follow her to the door. I have to witness this so I can tease her for the rest of the night.

Peeking through the small glass window in my door, I watch the three bikers turn their heads as Mya makes her way down the path towards the outdoor bin. She pays them no attention as she sways her arse. And as she walks back towards the house, she yelps and then hops, gripping one foot in her hand. One of the biker's races over to her, showing concern as he checks her foot. Mya looks up towards me, knowing I'm watching, and she winks as she holds on to the biker's shoulder.

I open my door, "Oh Mya, did you hurt your foot on those invisible stones that cover my path?" I ask sarcastically. Mya scowls and the biker laughs, standing up straight.

"Siren, come and meet my brother's," shouts Griffin, from his garden.

"No," I shout back, "Get in here, you fraudster," I add to Mya.

"Oh, so you're Siren," smirks the biker that Mya is still clinging to. He lets his eyes run down my body.

"No, I'm Neve," I say firmly.

"I'm Knox. Come and meet the guys, we're having a housewarming for Griff. Come and have a drink."

"No, I'm good. Thanks anyway."

"Neve," hisses Mya, "Don't be rude. Let's go and meet your new neighbour."

"You do remember what happened the last time you introduced me to someone right?" I remind her.

"Get over it, you got a gorgeous daughter out of it," smiles Mya, hooking arms with the biker and letting him lead her over towards my new neighbour. I sigh and glance down at my shorts and vest. It isn't party attire and I really do want an early night, but I don't want to leave Mya with a bunch of strangers.

Chapter Two

Neve

By the time I reach Griffin's garden, which is now filled with bikers and the odd female companion, Mya is nowhere to be seen. I contemplate going back home. She's obviously occupied, but then if something bad happened to her, I'd feel awful.

"Siren you came," says Griffin, approaching me with open arms and that wide smile that tells me he's full of fun and cheek.

"My friend left me no choice, did you see where she went?" I ask, glancing around.

"She'll be off somewhere with Knox. Don't worry, he'll take good care of her and return her in almost new condition," he says with a wink. He passes me a bottle of beer, twisting the cap off in front of me, "Opened in front of you so you know I'm not a date rape kind of guy."

"You know, you just saying that makes you creepy," I point out, taking the beer.

"You need to chill a little Siren, you're so uptight and snappy all of the time, anyone ever tell you that?" asks Griffin, drinking back his own beer.

I keep a neutral expression on my face. I've been told that a lot, and I hate that it bothers me so much. I can't help but be guarded, the last time I let my hair down, I fell in love with a sadist. But I wasn't always this way, I used to be carefree and relaxed around everyone. I was the type of girl to chat to anyone and make everyone feel welcome. I watch Griffin walk off towards a group of women, and I suddenly feel alone and like a total bitch. Griffin is always nice to me, and yet I'm so rude back.

I make my way through the house, pushing through the crowd of people and heading out to the back garden. It's quieter out here, with just a few people chatting near the patio. I sit down on the small wall and take a sip of beer.

Griffin comes bounding out of the house and glances around, "Anyone seen Ryder?" he shouts out, and a guy nearby points down to the bottom of the garden. I watch Griffin head in that direction, and sure enough, I make out a shadowy figure sitting under the large tree. Griffin stays to chat with the shadow for a few minutes, and then heads back towards the house, he catches sight of me and smirks, "You should go sit with Ryder, he's up tight like you."

I stand abruptly, "I am not up tight, you don't even know me."

Griffin approaches me with his cocky smile firmly in place. "Prove it." He raises his pierced eyebrow, "Do something crazy and totally not like you, go and kiss Ryder."

I groan out loud, shaking my head at his childish suggestion. "What are you, twelve?"

He grins and continues back towards the house. "See, you're uptight, Siren. You can't even stand the thought of letting yourself loose. You might actually like it." I scowl as he disappears inside. I don't just kiss random strangers, that doesn't make me uptight, it makes me sensible.

I glance back at the shadow under the tree and decide I may as well head down there and see if this Ryder guy is uptight, he's probably just as nice as me, and it's actually just Griffin being a complete dick. I make out his large frame as I get closer, his shoulders are wide and muscly, as is his chest. The tight white T-shirt he's wearing clings to each toned pec and I have to force my eyes to move up to his face. His arms are hung over his knees which are raised, and he holds a beer bottle loosely in his large hand. He fixes me with his electric blue eyes and I almost sigh out loud, he's totally gorgeous. Even hotter than Griffin.

"I'm Neve," I blurt out. His expression remains the same, his eyes pinned to my own. "I live next door to Griffin," I add, shifting uncomfortably under his intense stare. I wait for a few seconds, but again, he doesn't speak. "And I realised tonight that he's a complete arse. He called me up tight," I say, lowering to the ground to sit beside him and ignoring the fact he's made no indication he wants to talk to me. "I'm not uptight, I just find him over the top, like a bouncy puppy dog that doesn't stop," I continue, now trying desperately to fill the awkward silence with pointless chatter. "My ex called me uptight, so Griffin saying it kind of pissed me off. Then he said you were uptight so I thought I'd come and say hi, maybe we could rename this the uptight tree?" I say, with a small laugh. "The last thing I wanted tonight was to come to a party. Does that make me uptight? I'd rather sit in and wait for my ex to call so that I can hear my daughters voice, than hang out with a gang of criminals getting drunk. My friend dragged me here because she's been single for at least a month, that's way too long in Mya's eyes. I'd rather stay single for the rest of my life, it's easier like that." I realise I'm rambling on, my words pouring from my mouth one after the other with hardly a breath in between, but the guy still doesn't chip in or speak. And now I'm too intrigued to just get up and walk off. I need to know what his voice sounds like, half hoping it's high pitched and squeaky, somewhat like Pee Wee Herman's, at least then he wouldn't be so perfect. Because right now, sitting there with a brooding silence around him, he's coming across as dangerous and hot. "Anyway, sorry to have bothered you. I don't usually talk to strangers, I've only had two drinks and I'm talking complete bollocks." I stand, brushing the back of my shorts. His eyes follow the action, but he remains silent, and so I head back to the house feeling disappointed he didn't engage with me. My mind is already trying to make me believe he's some brooding, perfect hero, that'll sweep me off my feet. *I really need to stop reading those romance novels.*

I make my way upstairs. Griffin's house is the same layout as my own, so I find the bathroom with no problem and I'm relieved to find it empty. Once I'm finished, I step out on to the landing, debating whether to just leave and text Mya explaining. I notice the lights are now off, which is bizarre, because I'd definitely turned them on when I came upstairs minutes ago. I feel my way along the landing, and yelp when my hand presses against a man's hard chest. "Sorry," I squeak out. Before I can pass, a large hand wraps around my wrist and spins me around so that I'm facing the wall. An arm goes around my waist and lifts me effortlessly, holding me against his body tightly. Another hand presses against my mouth. He carries me forward and I hear a door open. I'm lowered to the ground, but the hand remains over my mouth. Strangely, I don't feel scared, in fact, I actually feel turned on. But before I can examine my thoughts on that, I feel his hot breath on my neck and he murmurs, "You come across as uptight, but you aren't. You have the same needs as every woman, you just don't know how to ask for it. If you want to fuck me, you have to ask me straight." The low voice rumbles in my ear. Instead of fear or outrage swallowing me, I feel a shiver of pleasure. "Your body gave me all the right signals. The lip chewing, the hair fiddling, the legs pressing together to ease the throbbing."

I inhale sharply. "I didn't mean..." I trail off when he presses his lips against my neck and runs little kisses against the sensitive skin there. I press my hands to the wall and close my eyes, enjoying the way his hard body feels against my back.

"Don't insult me by saying I imagined it," he growls, nipping my skin and causing sparks to ignite right down to my toes. His hands run down my arms and then trail under my vest, gently stroking my stomach. When I don't stop him, he moves higher, cupping my breasts and gently tugging my nipples. "Enough talking," he whispers, spinning me to face him.

He lifts my shirt over my head and drops it to the ground, then expertly unclips my bra. His mouth finds my nipple and he sucks it into his warm mouth. I cry out, grabbing onto his shoulders and throwing my head back in pleasure, it's been too long since a man's touched me like this and it feels amazing. His hand slips into the waist band of my shorts. He groans when he touches my knickers, "You're wet," he growls, before slipping a finger beneath the material, and running it along my opening.

"If you want me to stop you need to tell me now, because if you don't, I'm fucking you quick and hard." Something in his words sends sparks shooting to the spot he's now stroking. I remain silent, too lost in pleasure to speak. "Don't say I didn't warn yah," he mutters, close to my ear. He lifts me up and I wrap my legs around his waist, shamelessly rubbing myself against him. He fiddles around between us, loosening his belt and opening the button on his jeans. I hear him rip a condom wrapper open and a minute later, he moves my shorts to one side and presses the head of his erection to my opening. I've never had a one-night stand, it usually takes me a few dates before I'd ever consider getting intimate, but something about this man sends me wild, and all I can think about his how great I feel with his hands hungrily touching me and his mouth tasting my skin. He eases himself in slow, an inch at a time, giving me chance to adjust to his size. Once he's as far as I can take him, he stills, resting his head against my shoulder and panting like he's in pain. "Fuck, you feel good," he groans. I wiggle impatiently and he hisses. "Unless you want this to be over with in a second, you gotta let me lead," he warns, kissing my neck. When he finally begins to move, it's like pleasure I've never felt. I'm full, stretched in ways that Finn never achieved, and the faster Ryder moves, the more that warm feeling builds up in the pit of my stomach. I grip his shoulders so tight; I feel my fingernails digging into his flesh. He places his hand between our sweaty bodies and begins to rub circles over my swollen clit. I shiver against him, and then the orgasm rips through me, sending me spiralling. White spots fill my eyes and a scream escapes me as I shuddered uncontrollably. Ryder sucks the skin on my collar bone, his breaths becoming uneven and laboured. "I wanna taste you so fucking bad," he pants. Then he stills, growling as he releases into the condom. He slowly moves back and forth, as his orgasm subsides. Then, before I can move, he lowers to his knees, gripping one of my thighs, and pushing my legs apart. I'm so entranced watching this strong man kneel before me, that when he swipes his tongue along my opening, I cry out in surprise, sliding my fingers into his hair. He growls again, pushing his mouth against me and torturing me in the most delicious way, until I come apart again.

An awkward silence follows our intimate moment, as Ryder disposes of the condom into a tissue while I dress quickly. I'm not sure on the rules for one-night stands, or what the etiquette is afterwards, but when I catch a glimpse of Ryders face in the moonlight streaming through a small window, it tells me I need to say my goodbyes and get the hell out of there. I've heard horror stories of men giving women the wrong phone number just to get away, I don't want that awkwardness.

I run my fingers through my hair before reaching for the door handle. I still when his hand covers mine and he presses against my back. A spark of hope ignites in the pit of my stomach, maybe I've read him wrong, maybe he wants to see me again. "Let me go first in case any of the ol' ladies are out there."

I have no idea who he means when he says ol' ladies, but I'm guessing it's some kind of girlfriend. I instantly feel terrible. And I can't deny I'm slightly disappointed, they weren't the words I wanted to hear. I move to one side, letting him pass me. He turns back, giving me an awkward smile, "Give it a minute before you follow, the club girls might be out there," he adds, before leaving.

I feel humiliated, if that's how one-night stands work, then I'm going to leave it to experts like Mya, because yes, I'd felt a moment of pleasure, well maybe more than a moment; but it wasn't worth the feeling of being used straight afterwards. He couldn't even look me in the eye before he left. And the fact he wants me to hide out in here while he makes his escape, feels even worse, like he's embarrassed to be seen with me.

Chapter Three

Neve

I wait two minutes before heading back down the stairs. I find Mya in the hall chatting to another guy. She looks up at me and smiles, "Where have you been, I was looking for you," she asks.

"I got side tracked, everything okay?"

Mya eyes me suspiciously but decides not to push. "I got a call from Finn, he's angry because you didn't answer your phone," she explains. Panic fills me and I soon forget my humiliation. Finn's the kind of man to jump in his car and come to find me and I can't risk that, when he's got Harlee in his care. I didn't bring my mobile with me because I was caught off guard with this party that I didn't even want to come to. Mya reads my mind and holds out her mobile for me to use. I smile gratefully and rush out to the back garden to make the call. I move to the corner away from anyone else and dial Finn's number. I know it off by heart because of the need for me to check in constantly when we were still together. Not that it's really changed too much, he still expects the same and for a quiet life, I do it.

Finn answers within the first two rings, he doesn't speak, just connects the call and waits for me to explain myself. It's all part of his mind games.

"Finn, is everything okay? Is Harlee okay?" I ask, unable to hide the worry from my voice.

"Where are you, Neve?" he grates out.

"I'm having drinks with Mya, I told you that earlier."

"I spoke to Mya, she didn't know where the hell you were," he yells. I flinch at the volume of his voice.

"Look I'm not going to argue with you, Finn. Put Harlee on so I can talk to her."

"Don't dictate your demands to me, Harlee went to bed upset because her mummy wasn't around to talk to her. Were you with another man?" I check my watch, it's only seven in the evening, Harlee wouldn't be asleep yet, bedtime's usually half past seven and then she demands at least three stories before she'll snuggle down to sleep.

"You're only spiting Harlee by not letting me talk to her. No wonder she didn't want to come to you. Did you manage to spend time with her today?" I ask, ignoring his question. Finn laughs. He's trying to throw me off the subject, meaning he didn't spend time with her at all. "Enjoy the rest of your evening, I'll bring Harlee back at *some* point tomorrow."

Panic takes hold of me. "No, Finn, the agreed time is noon. I promised her I'd watch movies with her."

"Well you also promised to answer my phone call so you could speak to her. Jenifer is now having to spend time consoling our daughter because of you. I don't need to remind you of what will happen if your shoddy behaviour continues around my daughter."

I frown. I haven't heard the name before, "Jenifer, who the fuck is Jenifer?" I demand, beginning to pace back and forth in frustration. We'd agreed to keep new partners away from Harlee until they were established relationships. We also said we'd tell each other about new partners so we could work out when to tell Harlee, together. I didn't like the idea of introducing Harlee to people that wouldn't stick around for long.

"Goodnight, Neve. And don't forget the picture, or there will be issues with me returning her at all tomorrow." I take deep breaths to calm myself, blinking fast so that angry tears don't spill down my cheeks. I continue to pace back and forth after the call, keeping my hands on my hips and my head hung low. I'm so tired of his threats but he's a lawyer and he knows all the right things to say to make me comply.

"Is that lover boy checking up on you?" Ryders rumbling voice startles me and I spin to look at him, my face flushing slightly when our eyes connect. I assumed he'd left.

"No," I reply bluntly, my guard back up in place.

"I'm assuming you want to keep it on the downlow if you've just cheated. I'd also appreciate it if you didn't tell my brother, he'll get all stupid about it."

I inhale an angry breath, *what is it with men treating me like crap just lately?* "Firstly, I've never cheated on anyone in my life. That was my very first and very final one-night stand. Secondly, I don't have a clue who the hell your brother is, so I won't be telling him nor anyone else for that matter, I'm not the kind of girl to gossip especially about myself." I stomp away, not sticking around to wait for his reply.

I pass Mya in the hallway, "I'm going home. You coming?" I ask, holding out her phone.

She takes it and smiles. "Sure, let me just say goodbye to..." she trails off, looking at the man.

"Bear," he answers for her. I roll my eyes, Mya never seems embarrassed by her brazen ways.

"You did what!" screeches Mya glaring at me in shock. I'd blurted out my surprise one-night stand with the mysterious Ryder, as soon as I'd closed my front door.

"I wanted to prove to myself that I wasn't uptight, I know it sounds stupid, but I wanted to live a little."

"And you thought you'd have sex with the motorcycle gang leader?" Mya laughs.

"Leader?" I repeat, "I thought he was just friends with Griffin. Is he important? Oh my god is he some kind of criminal mastermind, cos I'll be honest with you, I thought he was a mute at first."

"He's the club president. I don't know how it all works but he's a tough guy, he's got a lot of respect amongst the others," Mya explains.

"They're in a gang?" I ask. "Oh God, is Griffin dangerous? I don't want them next door if they are."

"Relax, they're harmless."

"I guess it doesn't matter now anyway. He was good for my first one-night stand, but I won't be doing that again. How do you do it? I felt so used," I groan, making Mya laugh out loud.

"Neve, you're so innocent." She shrugs. "You go into it knowing you just need one thing, don't expect any more," she explains, "That way, you don't feel used or let down afterwards."

I don't know how to turn my emotions off like that, isn't sex about feelings and love? Without those, it feels cheap and dirty. "I did go into it knowing that, actually I didn't even have chance to think about it, he kind of ambushed me. But it was the way he acted afterwards that threw me. He must have women falling at his feet looking the way he does with all that brooding manliness, and he made me feel like I was a dirty secret that he regretted instantly. He said something about not wanting club girls and ol' ladies finding out?" I pour us both a large glass of white wine and pass one to Mya.

"Women that hang around and keep the guys satisfied if you know what I mean, most of them hope to get a husband out of it, become ol' ladies to the guys, but most don't ever get that."

"What are ol' ladies?"

"Women they make theirs. Like a wife I guess. If a biker claims his ol' lady, she's treated with respect by all members and protected by the club."

"You're like a mind of knowledge, how do you know all this? I have zero knowledge on motorcycle gangs let alone all their gang terminology."

"I read books," Mya replies.

"I don't believe for one second that you read," I tease, "Anyway I'm gonna hit the sack, I'm exhausted," I say on a sigh. I drain the wine. "Are you staying over?"

She shakes her head and smiles. "I might pop back next door for a while, it's still early to us single, non-parent girls."

I climb into bed and reach for my mobile phone. I take a picture, just a headshot, showing my pillow in the background. I send it to Finn to appease his incessant need to know where I am. Within seconds my phone lights up with an incoming call from Finn. I sigh before accepting the call. If I ignore him, he'll just keep trying. "Are you alone?" he asks, and I roll my eyes.

"Of course."

"Video call me, I don't believe you," he snaps, disconnecting the call.

"For goodness sake," I mutter out loud to myself. I video call him straight back. He smirks, pleased he's still controlling me. "See, all alone," I mutter, moving the phone to show the room.

"Good. See you tomorrow."

I get woken early the next morning by someone outside, screaming and laughing. I sit up quickly, alarmed by the noise and dive from my bed to look out the window. There's a group of people next door having a water fight. Griffin is running around topless, chasing my best friend around his garden with a jug of water. Mya screams as the water hits her, soaking her shirt through.

In the doorway of the house is Ryder, and wrapped around him is a female with long blond hair, short denim cut offs and a bikini top. Her legs and arms are wound tightly around him like a baby chimp clinging to its mother. He still has that blank look about his face. Suddenly, Ryder glances up at my window, almost like he felt me staring. We briefly lock eyes before I step back out of view, mortified that he's caught me.

I tap my fingers impatiently on the tabletop. Finn was supposed to return Harlee over two hours ago. I've tried numerous times to contact him, but to no avail. And I know he'll bring her eventually, but I can't relax until he does. Mya bursts in through the front door, a happy smile on her face. One look at me wipes that smile, "Are you okay?" she asks with concern.

"No, Finn hasn't brought Harlee back," I mutter.

"Wow that man is such an arse hole. I take it you called him?" She turns on the coffee machine and grabs a cup.

"Yep, no answer."

"Well look, you know he'll return her, he's just playing games again. Ignore him. Seriously, the man doesn't want to have Harlee at all, we both know he takes her just to annoy you. He will bring her back." As she finishes her words, the sound of a car engine stopping outside has me rushing to the door. Finn's car is out front with Finn in the driver's seat and a blond woman unstrapping Harlee from the back seat. I glare at Finn angrily, he winds down his window and rests his elbow there, a picture of calm.

"Where the hell were you, Finn, she was supposed to be back two hours ago."

"And you were supposed to answer your phone last night," he says sternly, removing his shades and giving me a pointed stare. I watch the blond lift Harlee from the car seat and hold her on her hip while she closes the car door. Her tight purple dress clings to her curvy frame and I find herself wondering if she's had breast and arse implants. She totters on her high black heels, handing Harlee over to me with a kind smile.

"Hey baby girl, I missed you," I whisper, placing tiny kisses all over her face.

"Finnegan, how totally not lovely to see you," says Mya, stepping out beside me and smiling sarcastically.

"Mya, still a bitch I see," he retorts.

"Wow look at this piece of arse, did you pay for her to look this good for you?" Mya asks with a grin, pointing to the blond.

"We need to talk about this," I cut in, "We said no introducing Harlee to new relationships, Finn."

"Harlee loves Jenifer, don't you bunny," Finn smiles awkwardly at our daughter, and I wonder why it doesn't come naturally to him to love her, the way I do.

"That isn't the point, Finn, and you know it. I'll call you later so we can talk about this."

"Oh sweetie, what have you let yourself in for," Mya asks Jenifer, with a fake concern, "Don't you have parents that love you, that want the best for you? Because honey, he is not it and I feel like I should be the one to warn you under girl code or some shit, that this man," she says, pointing towards Finn, "Is a complete bastard."

Finn gets out of the car abruptly, slamming his door. "Shut the hell up bitch, I never liked you," he growls, making a beeline for Mya. Harlee snuggles into me, burying her face into my neck. It's a well-practised move I taught her, to avoid her seeing the anger in Finn.

Mya laughs and steps closer to Finn to show him she isn't scared. "Well, that's great because I never liked you either, you bullying piece of shit," she snarls.

"Is there a problem here?" comes Griffin's voice, and he saunters across the garden towards us, looking the picture of calm. "Because the body language ain't great from where I was watching," he adds, his eyes firmly fixed on Finn.

"Wow the great Eric Griffin Fenton," Finn says with a smirk, "How's your brother? I heard he got out early, was he a good boy or did he bend over for the guards and get a deal?"

Griff's eyes change and I see the subtle switch, telling me that things are about to turn to shit. I pass Harlee to Mya and move in front of Griff. "Go back inside Griff, this is my business."

"Your cards are marked. Ryder has a long memory, and you'll regret making him your target," he spits.

"Please don't threaten me. I'm not scared of you or your little gang," snaps Finn, and then he turns his anger on me, "And you, you'd better call me tonight or I'll be turning up for a little visit." I watch him get back into his car, Jenifer rushes to join him and he drives away at speed.

"Arsehole," mutters Griff.

"How do you know him exactly?" I ask, reeling from the fact that Griffin had just confirmed that Ryder was his actual blood brother.

"He's the most dishonest lawyer I've ever met and trust me I've met a few. Screwed my brother over and got him sent down for something he didn't do. Ryder's gonna make his life a misery."

"Starting with me?" I ask, wondering if that was the reason Ryder slept with me last night. All the pieces begin slotting into place.

Griff gives me a blank stare, clearly not understanding me. "Look, we're having a cookout at the clubhouse this evening. Kids welcome. Just a fun get together, why don't you and Mya come, bring Harlee, she'll love it."

"Yeah we'll be there," I answer, without hesitation. I'll get answers from the man himself because I need to make it clear he's not using me in his game against my ex.

Chapter Four

Ryder

I'm tired, since getting home yesterday afternoon, I've been on the go and I'm regretting it. And now my brothers have decided to throw me a welcome home party. I pop a couple of caffeine tablets and swallow those down with a can of energy drink. After five years inside I have a lot of partying to do and a lot of debts to settle, I can't do that if I'm sleeping.

I shower quickly and pull on a fresh white t-shirt and some clean jeans. I'm grateful that Griff had sent one of the old ladies to get me some new clothes. None of my old stuff fits. When I first went inside, I didn't bother with weights or the gym, but being in prison changed me. With nothing better to pass the time, I worked on myself. I sorted out my diet and hit the gym hard. Five years on, I look more like the hulk and I'm proud of my hard work.

I head straight for the club bar, if there's one thing I missed, it's a good whiskey. The guys inside had alcohol brought in, but it wasn't the same as sitting with my brother's and drinking it from a glass instead of a mug. Bear grins at me from behind the bar. He places my favourite bottle and glass at my usual spot on the bar. I take it, thanking him with a fist bump, and then I head outside to where Griff has set up inflatables for the kids and seating areas for the adults. Smokey is on the grill cooking steaks and laughing with my brother. As I approach, Griff grins, "Brother, we were just talking about Mya," he smirks. The short haired beauty had been hanging around my brother all night and trying her best to get in his bed. But it wasn't Mya currently taking up space in my head. It was her gorgeous friend. The brunette with the long hair and a bright smile. Her green eyes and her perfect figure had my blood racing. And when I think about the way she tasted, I shudder.

"Oh yeah, what about her?" I ask, sipping my whisky.

"I invited her, but Bear reckons she won't turn up," says Griff.

"Why'd you invite her?" I ask, wondering if she'll bring her friend. They both look past me, leaving my question unanswered and when I turn to see what's caught their attention, I'm faced with the hot woman I've been thinking about since being inside of her less than twelve hours ago. My heart beats a little faster and I laugh at myself getting giddy like a fucking schoolboy. I put it down to the fact she was my first since going inside.

As she marches over, with her friend in tow, she fixes me with a glare and puts her hands on her hips. "Did you use me last night?" she demands to know.

I'm taken back and I hear my brothers sniggering, enjoying the fact I'm being called out by a woman in my own club. I frown. "That's the point of a one-night stand, darlin'."

"I mean, did you fucking use me to get back at Finn?" she says, her voice slightly raised. I only know one Finn and I'm pretty sure we're not talking about the same guy. "Because Griff said you wanted pay back, was I the payback?"

"Are we talking about Finnegan Lawrence?" I ask, praying to god she isn't.

"Yes," she snaps impatiently, "Did you fuck me to get at my husband?"

My world tilts for a second, her words hitting me hard. I've unknowingly fucked Finnegan's wife. A smile forms on my lips, and before I can explain anything, she slaps me hard across the face. All kinds of emotions run through me as the pain stings my cheek. It's been a while since I've been hit in the face by a woman, I'd forgotten what that burn felt like, and an even longer while since I've killed someone for disrespecting me, mainly because people don't disrespect me, ever.

Griff comes between us. "Fuck Siren, what the hell was that?"

I move Griff out of the way and step closer, using my size to intimidate her. I force her to back up until she hits the wall. "Do you know what I normally do to people that disrespect me in front of my brothers?" I growl, close to her ear.

She shakes her head and I see fear in her eyes. I get the sudden urge to fuck her against this wall and be damned if everyone can see, but a little voice catches my attention.

"Mummy are you okay?" I look down at a small girl with long brown hair, a slight curl in the ends, her green eyes looking between Neve and me.

I step back and Neve swoops the little girl up into her arms and carries her away, without a backwards glance. Griff approaches me smirking, "Jesus what was that?" he asks, "You fucked her last night?"

"She had something to prove, and I had some time to make up for," muttered Ryder, "She thinks you're an arse by the way," I add.

"Well I am, you're the bigger arse though, but she'll find that out herself," says Griff, patting me on the back. "I was gonna tell you about Finn by the way, looks like she beat me to it."

"Yeah, thanks for the heads up."

He laughs. "I was giving you a few days to settle in before we talked about that piece of shit."

He's right, even the name brings dark thoughts to my head.

I sit on a large boulder staring hard into the flickering orange flames of the fire pit. Neve is across from me talking to Griff. Her daughter is in her arms, draped around her like a baby monkey, and Mya is by her side.

It annoys the hell out of me that Neve was married to that arse. How can someone like her have fallen for an evil, twisted shit bag like him?

I stand, making my way over to the group. Griff smiles, fist bumping me. "Things good Pres?" he asks, I nod then turn to Neve.

"Follow me," I say. I need to be alone with her.

She scowls stubbornly. "Really, does that work on women?" she snaps, and I stare at her blankly. "You just order women around, and they do it because your what..." she pauses, "The boss around here?"

"No, they do it because I've killed for less. Now move it." I love her fire and the way she challenges me, it sends a thrill through me.

Neve hands her daughter to Mya, and for a second, I think she's actually going to follow me without giving me anymore grief. But she folds her arms over her chest. "No. I'm talking and you didn't say please."

"Did you just tell me no?" I ask, feeling mildly irritated. Usually women fall at my feet, they don't refuse me, ever.

"Respect my right to say no to you, you're not the boss of me and I'm not scared of you."

I roll my eyes. "Fucking new age women. I just want to talk and you've got to make it a big deal with your women's rights bullshit." Then I surprise her by lifting her up and throwing her over my shoulder. She cries out in shock and Mya tries to object but with the kid sleeping in her arms, she gives up the second I begin striding away towards the clubhouse. I don't stop until I have her safely in my office where I plant her feet back on the ground as I lock the door.

"How the hell dare you..." she begins, her face full of rage. I grip her chin between my finger and thumb roughly, and I kiss her. It stops her ranting instantly, and I pull back giving a satisfied smile.

"I can't get you off my fucking mind," I whisper against her lips. "I need to be inside you." I slam my mouth over hers again, and this time, she wraps her arms around my neck.

I release myself from my jeans, that're practically choking my erection. I take a condom from my pocket without breaking our kiss, rip it open and pull it down over my cock. I inch up her flowing cotton dress and move her underwear to one side, lining myself at her entrance. I don't have the patience to wait, the second her wetness touches me, I push into her, taking her by surprise. She grips my biceps, holding on tight as I thrust hard, each time trying to get deeper. I groan, pushing my face into her neck. She feels like heaven and I can't control the urge to come. "I gotta change position," I whisper. "Or we ain't both gonna reach the end here." She smirks as I withdraw my cock and bend her over my desk.

"Why did you marry that dick head?" I ask, slamming back into her with urgency.

"You want to discuss my bad choices right now?" she asks, looking back at me over her shoulder. Fuck she's sexy with that flustered look on her face.

"Is there anything between you?"

"No," she pants, pressing her forehead against the desk and shuddering with pleasure. "I'm not a cheat." She cries out, orgasming right before I follow her over the edge.

The only sound in the room, as I pull out of her and dispose of the condom, is our heavy breaths. She adjusts her clothes and I tuck myself away. That just fucked look suits her, making me want to bury myself in her all over again. I sit at my desk. "So," I say. "Tell me about you and Finn."

Neve

"There's nothing to tell. We married and then we split up." Finn's the last person I want to talk about right after we just did what we did.

"You ain't leaving here until we've talked, Neve, so drop the attitude."

He makes me feel like I'm a teenager in trouble. I sigh heavily. "I married him, he was an arse. I had his child and then he disposed of me, preferring to fuck about than deal with me." I notice the way Ryder lifts his brow, like he understands why Finn would do that. "I'm a nice person," I snap defensively. "But since him, I don't like being bossed around. You want to talk to me, just ask."

"Noted." He sighs, rubbing at his forehead and looking stressed.

"You really should get some sleep, Ryder, you look exhausted." I bite my lower lip, contemplating whether to ask my next question. I can't keep having sex with this man when I have no idea who he really is or how dangerous he is. "What did you go to prison for?"

He's not going to tell me. I see by the way his expression changes. "Get out."

I roll my eyes. "Wow, nice manners. Yah know, a little courtesy wouldn't hurt after we just hooked up . . . again."

"If you keep disrespecting me like you do, we're gonna have a real problem," he mutters, coldly.

I laugh, "Oh really?" I ask, "I was always taught that to get respect, you have to show respect, and seeing as so far, you haven't shown me an ounce, then you can expect the same!" I stomp from his office, slamming the door behind me for good measure.

Mya stands as I approach. "Are you ready to go now?" she asks. I nod, taking Harlee from her and heading to the car without a word.

Mya decides to sleep at mine, something she often does seeing as her roommate is always bringing home random one-night stands. So when we get home, I put Harlee straight to bed and make up the spare room for Mya.

"Are you going to tell me about you and Ryder?" she asks, leaning against the door frame as I lay the final blanket on her bed.

I shake my head. I'm exhausted. "Do you mind if we leave it for tonight?"

She nods, giving me a kiss on the cheek as I pass her to go, "Sure, but we do need to discuss it. You shouldn't look this stressed after great sex with a hot man." She sniggers and I roll my eyes.

"Goodnight."

I get into bed and video call Finn. He answers straight away, and I catch sight of Jenifer moving from the camera view as the call connects.

"Home alone," I say with a bored sigh. I move my phone around for Finn to see my room.

"Good," he replies, but before he could disconnect the call, I blurt out the one question I've never asked before, mainly because I don't actually care, but for once, I want to piss him off.

"Are you?"

Finn pauses, his brow furrowing. He's not used to being questioned, and he hates it, but I am sick to death of him holding all the cards. Maybe if I start being difficult, he'll back off.

"I don't have my daughter here, so it doesn't matter," he replies carefully. It's the reason he makes me do this fucked up call every night. He seems to think my duty as her mother, is to not have any life outside of parenthood.

"I didn't have her at the weekend yet I still had to call. So going by your own rules, means I can stop calling you at a weekend when I don't have Harlee here." I'm feeling smug and my expression must show it because he pushes to sit up, looking annoyed as he scowls at me through the screen.

"No, you're the mother of my child and so you should behave accordingly, with respect," he snaps.

"I've heard that word a lot tonight," I muse, thoughtfully. "How do you know Ryder?" This will definitely piss him off further but I'm feeling daring.

Finn's face goes a dark shade of red, the sort of colour he usually goes right before he loses his shit. I almost smile. "How do you know that name?"

"You saw that his brother moved in next door, right? He mentioned that you knew them both."

"Well ignore him and stay away, they're bad news. The last woman Ryder fucked, ended up dead."

Finn disconnects the call, leaving me staring at the blank screen. *Ryder killed someone?* I snuggle into my bed with that last sentence playing on my mind. It should terrify me into staying away, but actually, I don't think it does. He's a complete arse, but that seems to be my type. And the sex . . . fuck the sex is good. I smile to myself. I should completely avoid him. Of course I should. But as I close my eyes, I know our paths will cross again.

Chapter Five

Neve

"I don't want to go out, I want to watch a movie and enjoy a quiet glass of wine," I complain as Mya throws a bag containing a new dress, my way. She's insisting we go out but I know it'll only cause another argument with Finn and I'm really in no mood. He's been awful since our conversation about Ryder and every night when I call, he interrogates me to see if I've spoken to either of the biker brothers.

As if sensing why I'm so hesitant, Mya fixes me with a glare, "Stop letting him control you. He did that when you were together and now, he's doing it still. He's moved on and he expects you to stay home. Where is that woman that stood up to the big bad biker boss last weekend?"

"Ryder can't use my daughter as a pawn in his games, Finn can, and he does."

"Only if you let him. Come on Neve, *please*. Let your hair down and have some fun. It's just one night."

I end up agreeing, much to Mya's delight, and an hour later, we're in a wine bar waiting for our friends to join us. I drink three shots of Sambuca straight just to gain some confidence for the outfit Mya forced me to wear.

When the girls arrive, Liss greets me with a wide smile and kisses each cheek. "Neve it's so great to see you out for once." I've known Liss for almost as long as I have Mya. We all went to school together, but once we hit teenage years, Liss and I became enemies after she stole two of my boyfriends. For a while, we all stopped hanging out, but then Mya met Liss again when they both started working for the same firm and she was re-introduced to the group. We laugh about it now, but back then, I really hated her.

"Mya made me come," I say with a shrug.

"That's great Neve, so you didn't actually want to come?" Charleigh asks. She's the moodier of our group. Also, a single mother like me, only her ex left them high and dry the second he'd discovered Charleigh was pregnant. He doesn't bother to have contact with her or their son.

"Don't start Charleigh, of course she wants to be here," says Mollie, turning to me, "Don't you Neve?" Mollie is the peacekeeper of the group. She's quiet and sweet, a thinker, and someone that you can call upon if you need sensible advice.

"No actually I didn't, I wanted to enjoy a night home in my pyjamas and watch reruns of Sons of Anarchy," I say, "But, now I'm here with my girls, I'm glad," I add with a smile.

"Why watch Sons when you could have the real thing?" asks Mya with a raised eyebrow. All the girls turned to me with quizzical expressions. Since Finn, I've not shown interest in any man. I just don't need the drama.

"Thanks for that unhelpful comment, Mya, shall we get more drinks?" I ask, waving to get the barman's attention.

"Erm, no we should not. What is she talking about?" demands Charleigh.

"Nothing, we met some bikers, nothing to talk about," I say vaguely. I place an order for two bottles of wine.

"Oh please, that smug smile screams fuckery," laughs Mya taking one of the bottles and three glasses and making her way to the nearest table. I pay the barman, and then take the other bottle and glasses to where the girls are settling into chairs.

"So, continue," Liss urges eagerly, leaning forward while Mya pours the wine.

"She had sex with the head of the gang. They call him the president. He's hot. Mean. Moody. And did I mention H.O.T," Mya gossips.

"What," screeches Mollie horrified, "He's in a gang?"

"Not that sort of gang Molls, calm down," I say with a sigh, while patting her hand, "Mya is over selling it. A guy next door to me is in a motorcycle *club*. Most of the guys are ex-army and they have a place where they all get together so that they can still be part of a brotherhood."

"Well you seem to know a lot about them even though you say there is nothing to tell," smirks Liss.

"I googled it." I wink and she giggles.

"What was he in prison for?" asks Charleigh, "Is he safe to have around Harlee?"

"Jesus, I slept with the guy, we aren't getting married or anything. I have no idea why he was in prison, but I do know that I won't be seeing him again so you all just need to calm down and stop getting over excited. Besides Mya, didn't you spend the night at Griff's last weekend?"

All the girls turn to her and I give her a smug smile. She laughs. "Yeah but he's a total gent, nothing happened despite my efforts."

"Wow he resisted your charms?" teases Liss, with a laugh. Mya usually gets any man she wants, even the married ones.

I relax after finishing my second glass of wine, enough to get up and dance with the girls. I'm glad I decided to come out, because it feels good to be with the group of friends I've known for so long, I can't remember the last time I did this, especially with me and Charleigh both having childcare issues; it always makes plans more difficult to arrange. I haven't spoken to my parents since I told them I was marrying Finn. They'd never liked him and made it perfectly clear that they didn't approve of my choices. They live less than a twenty-minute walk away from my house, and I often think about reaching out to them. I know they'd love Harlee and would be more than happy to help me out when needed, but I guess I've become stubborn, and a part of me can't stand to let them know they were right.

I feel my mobile phone vibrate and I pull it from my bag, groaning when I see Finn's name. I wave my phone at Mya to indicate I have to take a call, before heading outside. "Is Harlee okay?" I ask, when I answer.

"Where are you?" he demands. I take a few more steps away from the bar, hoping it'll dim the background noise.

"Is Harlee still up? It's very late," I ask. The alcohol is making me braver and after our recent conversation, I'm determined to make him see that his behaviour isn't reasonable and he doesn't own me anymore.

"Harlee is in bed. Where are you, Neve?" He's persistent.

"Then why are you calling me, Finn?" I ask. "You only really need to call me about Harlee."

"Are you actually being serious right now?" he growls, and I know he's trying to stay calm.

"If you don't need anything for Harlee, I'm going to hang up. Good night Finn," I say, disconnecting the call. I stare at the phone for a few seconds and then a grin spreads across my face. I did it. I stood up to him. A passerby glances up as I do a little happy dance and I grin wider. "I did it," I tell him, and he frowns. People in London tend to keep themselves to themselves. I laugh. "I fucking did it and it feels good."

"Is the happy dance because you saw me?" I spin around to the sound of Griff's voice and my eyes land on his smirking face.

"What are you doing here, are you following me?"

He laughs. "Nope your friend text me and asked if we fancied joining you for a drink, we were in the area so..."

"We?" I repeat, praying to God he doesn't mean Ryder. My heart slams harder in my chest and my eyes dart around trying to spot him.

"Me, Saul, Knox and Ryder. We had a job just up the road," Griff replies. I zone out the second he says Ryder's name. *He's here.* The elation I felt minutes ago, has turned to anxiety. I'm not sure how to act around him and I wasn't prepared to see him when I'm so drunk. *Fuck.*

Griff takes me by the hand and leads me back into the bar, all the while, sickness bubbles away in my stomach while I repeat the mantra, *I must not sleep with a gang leader. I must not sleep with a gang leader . . . again.*

We find our friends all together, gathered snuggly around our table. They're all chatting like long lost friends and I roll my eyes, grabbing hold of Mya who was balanced on the edge of the seat. She yelps but I lead her away from the group before spinning to face her. "What the hell were you thinking inviting bikers on a girls night out?" I hiss.

Mya pouts like I'm overreacting. "I thought it'd be nice to have some male attention."

I narrow my eyes before waving my hands around the packed-out bar. "And none of these men would do?"

"Not compared to these guys I mean look at them, just their sheer size alone is hot. They walked in, and people actually turned to stare," she says, her words laced with excitement. "And they sat with us. I felt like a celebrity." She fans her face with her hand and fake swoons.

"I wish you'd have spoken to me first, I really want to avoid Ryder."

She narrows her eyes. "Why?" she asks. "I mean, look at him." And to my horror, she points at him.

I slap her hand back down to her side. "Why are you pointing," I cry, glaring at her like she's lost her mind. "He's going to think I made you invite them here. He'll think I'm some kind of stalker."

"Jeez, relax would yah," she says. "If you're not interested, just stay away from him."

I give a slight nod. "Yeah, you're right. I can just avoid him."

"Besides, Liss has you covered," she adds and I follow her line of sight back to the table where Liss is laughing hard at something Ryder is saying to her. There's a small lift of his lip too which annoys me. *He never smiles at me.* Liss leans closers and whispers in his ear. I roll my eyes in irritation. *She never changes.*

Ryder

Liss tucks her hair behind her ear in a polished move. She laughs at my comment, despite it not being funny. I smirk. She's like a female version of myself and I'm okay with that, it means a night of fun. Her hair is a dark brown and piled into some kind of messy bun on her head, it suits her. Her makeup's heavy, which makes her brown eyes look almost black. And she's sexy and sultry, the sort of girl I go for. She also knows what she's doing. Her tactics for reeling in the opposite sex are polished and refined. She asks all the right questions to make her seem like she's interested in me, without prying too much.

I've had years of practise at assessing people in prison, and I notice the way she keeps flicking her eyes over to Neve. Liss is jealous of her. Without a shadow of a doubt, she wants what

Neve has. "Maybe you could take me for a ride sometime, I've never been on a motorbike before," she gushes with enthusiasm, bringing me back to the conversation.

"Sorry darlin' I don't put a lady on the back of my bike unless she belongs to me," I reply. I glance at Neve, she's staring down at her drink looking lost in thought. I can't deny my attraction to her is strong. She's not the sort I'd ever go for, although she's naturally beautiful, she's not full of lip filler or plastered in makeup and I like it. I like her.

"So, what would a girl need to do to belong to you?" asks Liss, flirtatiously.

"That's top secret, I'd have to have known you a lot longer than five minutes to disclose that," I reply with a wink.

Neve stands abruptly, "I need to dance," she announces to the table, even though everyone is in separate conversations and no one acknowledges her.

I smirk and as she goes to leave, I reach for her, taking her wrist gently and halting her. "Have I done somethin' to upset you?"

"I'm just trying not to offend you with my lack of respect again," she says, coldly.

I can't help but smile at her constant attitude. "You keep baiting me, you shouldn't." It's a veiled warning cos' I pray to the good Lord above she keeps up with her sassy mouth and bad attitude, fuck it turns me on.

"Whatever you say, Ryder," she mutters, pulling free and walking away.

Liss leans closer, placing her hand on my chest and smiling. "So where were we," she asks, and when I open my mouth to reply, she presses her red lips onto mine, flicking her tongue into my mouth in a bold move. *Yep, she's definitely jealous of Neve.*

Chapter Six

Neve

I glance over from my spot on the dancefloor to where Liss and Ryder are locked in a hungry kiss. I push down the feelings of jealousy, I have no right. And yeah, maybe sleeping with him *twice* should count for something in the girl code, but I doubt Liss gives a shit.

"Wow she didn't waste any time," Mya says as she joins me.

I shrug like I don't care. "She loves a bad boy."

"It's like school all over again. What was the guy you really liked and she just jumped right in there?" she asks, tapping her chin in thought.

"Dean," I reply, laughing, "And she didn't steal him, I let him go. Besides, Ryder's a free agent, it was just sex between us."

"At least he helped to break your dry spell," Mya adds.

I nod. "Always a Brightside."

A slow song comes on and Griff appears behind Mya, pulling her to him so she turns in his arms and hooks them around his neck. I notice some of the other bikers also joining the dancefloor with my friends so I head back to the table, feeling like a spare part. My step falters when I see Ryder is now alone. I consider passing him and heading for the bathroom but I don't want him to think I'm avoiding him because of his face-eating with Liss, so I take my seat and stare out at the dancefloor.

"No one to dance with?" he asks with a smirk.

"Not following Liss to the toilet for a quickie?" I retaliate, instantly regretting it because now he knows I'm bothered.

"We both know that I don't do quickies," he says, swirling his ice around in his tumbler of whiskey. "Where's your kid tonight?"

"None of your business."

"I was just wondering if you had an empty house is all," he asks, quirking his brow suggestively.

My heart rate picks up and I bite my lip to stop the smile I want to give him so badly. "I don't think that's a good idea after the way you blew up at me before, besides, you just stuck your tongue down my friends throat."

"She ain't a friend Siren, she wants what's yours."

I like the way he's stolen Griff's nickname for me. "You don't even know her and I didn't see you complaining."

"If you'd have watched for a second longer, you'd have seen me turn her down. I like my women a little less . . . desperate."

"I don't think you're fussy at all when it comes to women," I scoff.

"You're wrong. Just like you are about her. She's not a friend, Neve, and I'm willing to bet my bike that I'm not the first man she's gone after that you've had first."

My eyes dart down to where my hands fiddle with a broken beer matt. I don't want to call Liss behind her back, especially to a stranger. But before I can reply, he laughs, "I right aren't I, she's done that before." He leans back in the chair with a smug expression. "I sometimes surprise myself with my skills to read people."

"If you can read people so well, then you'd know I don't really want to talk to you right now."

He gives an easy grin, "Oh, Siren, I read you perfectly well. I'm so in tune with you, I can tell you exactly what you want from me right now." He leans closer again, resting his arms on the table and staring me in the eye. "You want me to lean across this table and kiss you." I laugh, shaking my head like he's being ridiculous. "Then you want me to drag you into a dark corner to fuck you hard and fast." I try to keep my breathing even so he doesn't know the effect his words are currently having on me. "And then you want me to take you home and worship every goddamn inch of your body with my mouth, right before I spend the night buried inside of you." I inhale sharply and his eyes darken with hunger. "So, I'm gonna ask you again Siren, where is that pretty little kid of yours tonight?"

"At her dad's," I say, noting how the words come out all breathy with need.

"Then what are we waiting for?" he asks, standing and holding out his hand.

I stare at it for a few seconds. "I can't...we aren't..." I stutter the protest out, shaking my head.

He takes my hand in his, and I marvel at the difference in size. "You can and we are," he says firmly He stands, still holding my hand in his, then he tugs me gently until I do the same. "Cos if I don't get you alone soon, I'm going to fuck you over this table. And the worrying thing is, I don't think you'd fucking mind."

Ryder fist bumps Griffin as we pass to leave. Mya smirks, winking at me but I'm too lost in my own head to respond and as he leads me from the club, I try to come up with all the reasons this is a bad idea. There aren't many, just one. Finn. And the optimist in me is screaming that I've already put Finn in his place and the world didn't break, so I can do this. I take a few deeps breaths. Besides, I like sex with Ryder. He makes me feel good and I deserve to feel good, right? I nod to myself, not realising Ryder has stopped and I crash into his back.

He turns to face me, smiling and I almost swoon. He should do it more. "Here," he adds, putting a helmet on the top of my head, then pushing it down until it's secure. He fastens a strap underneath my chin, then proceeds to put his own on.

A sound clicks inside of my helmet, making me jump in fright, and then Ryders voice crackles in my ear, "Get on." I watch him throw his own leg over, then glance down at my short skirt. He senses my worry and adds, "No one will see up your skirt, I'll be blocking their view."

I carefully climb on behind him and my skirt rides up. Ryder doesn't wait for me to try and adjust it, instead he grabs my thighs and yanks me closer. Then he finds my hands and wraps them around his waist until my face is pressed against his back. I turn it to the side. I've never been on a motorbike before, it was the one thing my mother always warned me about. "Hold tight," he tells me, right before a loud rumble fills the air, and a vibration runs through me, causing me to gasp. Ryder squeezes my bare leg, "Don't make those little noises, Neve, it does things to me."

As he pulls out into traffic, I squeeze my eyes closed in terror. The bike feels powerful as it rumbles and after a few minutes, I begin to relax, opening my eyes as Ryder expertly weaves in and out of the evening traffic. His voice crackles in her ear again. "I can feel your heat on my back, Neve. Are you wet for me or the bike?"

I feel my face burn with embarrassment. I'm not used to men speaking to me like Ryder does, but I must admit, I like it. "I've never been on a bike before," is all I can think to say.

"I've never had a woman on this bike, it's a first for both of us," he says, sliding his hand up my thigh. He continues until he's rubbing my inner thigh, causing me to open my legs a little wider. Then his finger brushes against my underwear and a moan slips out involuntary. The thought of him controlling this beast while touching me, sets me on fire. "I'm going to fuck you over my bike, Neve," he says, his voice rumbling through the headset. "I wanna taste you while you lay across her."

He slows the bike down, removing his hand and turning into my street. I take a deep breath to compose myself.

"Park outside Griff's place," I instruct, the last thing I need is Finn finding out about this before I've had chance to burn off some of this sexual chemistry. Ryder hesitates but does it anyway.

He places both feet on the ground and kills the engine. Then without warning, he reaches behind, scooping me in one hand and twisting me expertly around his body, until I'm on his lap and facing him. I'm so impressed by his slick moves, I don't realise what he's about to do until his hand is already hidden between us and he's moving my underwear to one side. He swipes a finger along my opening and I gasp, gripping my hands onto his shoulders. "Fuck, you're so wet," he growls, doing the same thing again.

"Jesus, Ryder, someone might see," I whisper.

He pushes his finger into me and I squeeze his shoulders tighter, leaning back slightly to give him easier access.

"They'll think it's my brother, you've got a helmet on," he says, adding a second finger. "Now come for me, Siren."

"I can't come here," I pant, even though my body is already feeling the lick of warmth.

He moves faster. "I bet you can, Siren. I bet you can come fucking hard on my fingers."

With the combination of his dirty words and the fact we're in public, it's mere seconds before I'm shuddering hard against his hand as an orgasm rips through me.

"See," he whispers, removing his hand. I lean back against the handlebars trying to regain control of my breathing as

Ryder takes off his helmet. I watch as he sucks his fingers into his mouth, licking them clean and humming in approval. "Now let's get inside so I can really taste you."

I get off the bike and remove my own helmet, passing it to him before scanning the street for any kind of life. "Relax," he says, also stepping off. "No one was watching. And if they did, they're probably getting off on us." I smile, but it doesn't reach my eyes. I'm not looking to see if the neighbours are curtain twitching. The reality of the way I spoke to Finn earlier is hitting me and I'm wondering if he's going to turn up.

Ryder doesn't give me too long to overthink before he's wrapping his arms around me and bustling me up the path to my front door where I fumble around in my bag for the keys. Once inside, he pushes me against the wall, kissing me hungrily and using his foot to kick the door closed.

I break the kiss, panting hard as I move past him to bolt the door. He watches, his eyes showing concern as I lock each of the five bolts before turning the key.

I smile, turning back to him and feeling more relaxed. "Safety first," I say with a shrug.

There's conflict in his eyes, he wants to ask me why I'm over cautious, but he changes his mind and grabs me, pulling me back to him and nuzzling his mouth against my neck. I feel sexy as he makes his way across my chest, kissing, licking, nipping, until he finds his way back to my lips.

In a bold move, I unfasten his belt, working the leather through the buckle quickly. I pull his zipper down and pop the button on his jeans. Both times we've had sex before, have been rushed and I haven't had a chance to feel him properly, it's something I've dreamed about since the last time and as I reach into his boxers and wrap my hand around his rock-hard shaft, I smile. He's huge. Bigger than I imagined. Ryder breaks the kiss, pressing his forehead to mine. His breathing is laboured, like my own and as I pump my hand up and down his shaft, he squeezes his eyes closed. "Fuck that feels good," he mutters.

I have this huge man in the palm of my hand, literally, and he's enjoying it. It makes me feel powerful and before I over think it, I sink to my knees and tug his jeans down to his ankles. The boxers follow and he springs free.

I was never any good at this sort of thing, Finn always told me so, but it still never stopped him making me do it. With Ryder, I want to do it. I have an insatiable need to taste him.

I wrap my hands around him and gently lick the end of his cock, letting the salty bead of precum, coat my tongue. His erection jumps in my hand and he lets out a low groan. It encourages me to do it again, this time wrapping my lips around the tip and taking him deeper into my mouth. His hands run through my hair and he groans each time he hits the back of my throat. "Fuck, Siren, that's the hottest thing I've seen in a long time," he murmurs and I look up, connecting my eyes to his. They're full of heat and promise and I suck harder, allowing him to grip the back of my head and guide me at the speed he likes. It's seconds before he's grunting and I feel his release hit the back of my throat. Somehow, it doesn't turn my stomach the way it used to with Finn. Ryder releases my head and holds out his hand, helping me to stand. He gently tucks some of my hair behind my ear and smiles. "What are you doing to me, Siren?" he almost whispers thoughtfully.

It suddenly feels awkward. I'm not sure what the next step is after a blow job on the hall floor. *Do we go and have sex?* If he's anything like Finn, he'll not be fit for anything else until tomorrow. "Coffee?" I ask and instantly wish the ground to open up and swallow me whole. Who the fuck offers a one night stand a coffee. He probably just wants to get the hell out of here.

Chapter Seven

Ryder

I smirk as her face reddens in that way it always does when she blurts something out without thinking it through and instantly regrets it. "I'd prefer a whiskey," I reply, tucking myself away and fastening my belt.

"I don't have alcohol in the house," she says, "Long story," she adds as an afterthought and I assume it's because she doesn't want me to probe further. And usually, I wouldn't. Why should I care what goes on in a chick's life? Once I get what I need, I walk away and never look back. Only with Neve, things are different. There's some kind of pull between us that can't keep me away. She isn't even my type, although lately, I don't even know what that is.

I follow her through to the kitchen and sit on a stool as she fills a glass with water and takes a few big gulps. I could have gone home with her friend, fucked her anyway I needed to, and been home in my own bed by now. But I had to feed the addiction for Neve. I craved her from the second Griff told me her friend had text him.

"We going to bed or are you planning to kick me out?" I ask and she almost chokes on the water. I've never stopped at a woman's house after any kind of sexual encounter. I'm a hit 'em and run kind of guy. Or at least I used to be, before I went inside. That shithole changed me, obviously.

"Erm, sure," she mutters, placing the glass in the sink.

I follow her upstairs, noting how clean her place is. Even the pictures of her little girl hang straight on the walls. I step inside her bedroom and raise my brows. It's the girliest room I've ever seen. Ever. And I've been in a lot of women's bedrooms. She watches me nervously, fidgeting with the hem of her top.

"It's very . . . pink," I say.

She smiles, also looking around at the soft pink walls adorned with butterflies and fairy lights. "I let Harlee choose the wallpaper," she admits. "And I hate to sleep in the dark." The last part almost slipped out and she bites her lower lip again. Occasionally, when she drops a secret like that, I want to push for more, but that would mean I feel something and so I push the urge to know down and shrug out of my leather kutte.

Neve watches as I place it carefully on a pink chair in the corner of her room. Next, I slip out of my heavy boots and place them equally as neatly beside the chair. When she still makes no move, I smirk. "Are you just gonna watch me undress?"

"You look so out of place in this pink room," she says, unable to stop her smile. "With your shaved head and all the . . ." her eyes run over my arms. "Tattoos. Maybe Liss would have been more your type. She's got a gothic theme running through her bedroom, all silk sheets and black . . ."

I don't let her finish that sentence, instead, I pull her to me, causing her to crash against me. She yelps. "I didn't want Liss. I wanted you. Again." I kiss her, running my hand into her hair and gripping it, gently tugging it while I let her tongue wrestle against mine. When I pull back, her eyes are darker, she's hungry for more. "In case you didn't notice, Siren, my body seems to only want you right now. And for the record, I don't ever go to bars that I don't own. I don't need to venture out to drink overpriced watered-down whiskey in dirty glasses; but when Griff told me about your friends little text, my mind couldn't stop thinking about you and what you'd be wearing," I pull back some more and look down at her outfit, "Which turned out to be very little. You keep pulling me back, Siren, and I don't know why I can't keep away, but I can't. So forget Liss, right now, all I want, is you."

The shrill of her mobile phone makes her freeze. The lust she had in her eyes seconds ago turns to something else, fear maybe? And she steps away, pulling her phone from the back pocket of her skirt. She stares at the screen before bringing her eyes back to me. "You're not going to understand this, Ryder, but I have to take the call from my ex and he can't know that you're here." There's a pleading tone to her voice and instead of questioning it, I nod my head once and move over to the bed.

Neve suddenly removes her top and replaces it with a pink pyjama one. The phone rings off. She then grabs a few wipes from a packet on her dressing table and makes quick work of removing her makeup. All the while, I don't ask questions and when the phone shrills again, she dives into bed and tussles her hair before answering.

"What?" she asks in a fake sleepy voice. I roll my eyes and turn my back to her, resting my elbows on my knees and staring down at the pink carpet.

"You're home then?" I hear Finn bark down the phone.

"Yes." "Show me," he demands. I glance back over my shoulder to her, wondering what he's asking her to show, and realise when she sweeps the phone to the empty space beside her, that he's checking she's alone.

"Explain what the fuck earlier was about?" he snaps.

"Sorry. I'd had a couple of drinks with my friends, I wasn't thinking."

"When are you going to realise that that gaggle of witches are not friends. You were so much better when you cut them from your life."

"I didn't cut them Finn, you stopped me seeing them," she mutters.

"And you were a much nicer person for it. I thought you'd want to know your daughter was a bitch tonight." Neve sits up straighter. "What do you mean?"

"She threw a tantrum for an hour straight at bedtime because she wanted you, have you poisoned my daughter against me?" he asks.

"No of course not. Is she okay? Why didn't you call me so I could speak to her?"

"Well you were too busy for calls weren't you, Neve," he tells her. "I gave her a good, slapped arse, like my father used to give me. She soon stopped playing up. You should try it, you're way too soft on her."

I bristle at his words. He's not a small guy and Harlee looks tiny. I squeeze my hands into fists, the urge to go find this piece of shit and hurt him is overwhelming.

"Jesus, Finn, you hit her?" Neve cries. "She's five years old."

"We're too soft on kids these days. We all had a slap or two when we were kids, it never hurt us."

"Times have changed. You should have called me, Finn. I can't believe you hit her. I think I should come and get her," says Neve, throwing her legs over the edge of the bed.

"Don't even think about it, Neve. You turn up here making a fuss and you'll get the same treatment. I seem to remember it working well on you." He disconnects the call and Neve throws the phone into the middle of the bed and buries her face in her hands.

This is a sign for me to walk away. Neve's obviously got issues and her ties to this wanker are going to cause me a headache I don't need, I have my own plans to mess with Finn Lawerence and she's not a part of that, but seeing her sobbing into her hands, does something to me inside and I find myself moving closer to her and wrapping her in my arms.

I wait for her to calm before turning her in my arms and forcing her to look at me. I place a finger under her chin, tipping her head back slightly. "What the fuck was that?" I ask, gently.

"I'm so sorry. I'm so embarrassed. I don't usually break down on hook ups," she sniffles.

Her words feel like a slap in the face and for some reason, they bother me way more than they should. "Hook up?" I repeat, "This is the third time we've ended up 'hooking up'" I say, using air quotes. "Don't you think it's a little more than that now?"

She eyes me warily, and then shrugs her shoulders. "I thought we were having fun."

I scoff, "Fun? I'm in your bedroom, Neve. I'm looking to stay the night, that's a huge deal for me."

Her expression softens and she rises onto her knees and places her arms loosely around my neck. "This doesn't feel fun at all right now, does it?" she whispers, trailing wet kisses over my neck. I tilt my head slightly, liking the feel of her against me again. "I need you, Ryder," she adds, bringing her lips to mine.

I allow it for a few seconds, my cock instantly hardens, but before she can distract me with her skilful mouth, I pull away and she falls back onto her arse. "Don't do that," I say, firmly. "Don't try and distract me. I want to know what the fuck that was."

Neve sighs heavily and crosses her legs. "You heard what that was, what do you want me to say?"

"I want you to tell me why the hell you even do any of that shit for him when you're not together." It crosses my mind that maybe there's more to them so I add, "Unless you and he are still fucking?"

"Don't be ridiculous," she snaps and I'm shocked at how relieved I feel to hear her say those words. "Look, I have a child with him and whether I like it or not, I have to keep the peace between us for her sake."

"And what about you, Neve? How often does he call to make you check in?"

She stares down at her hands and shame washes over her features. "Most nights . . . every night."

My fists ball at my sides in anger. "That can't go on. How the fuck will you ever move on?"

She looks me in the eye, "That's the whole point, isn't it. I can't."

I lay awake beside Neve's sleeping form. She's curled up in a tight ball with her back to me and I itch to wake her. She'd refused to talk about Finn anymore and instead turned on her distraction technique which led to her riding me until we both came hard. So I let her sleep, she needs the rest.

I go over my plan again, hating myself the more I think about it. When Griff first told me about her connection to Finn, I knew right away she was my key to ruining him. I want him to know how it feels to lose everything. And now that I know he's still hooked on her, it makes things all the sweeter. It would be so easy to go ahead. I have the recording of us fucking in my office, which I could easily send Finn's way . . . I groan, rubbing my hands over my tired face. How can I make her life worse? She's already living in hell because of Finn Matthews. The last thing she needs is me making shit worse. And besides, I like her. Way more than I ever meant to.

Neve stirs beside me, a small moan escaping her lips. She flinches and I wonder if she's dreaming about Finn. I turn, pressing myself against her and wrapping my arm around her. She settles, and I place a kiss into her neck. My erection strains against her backside, itching for another taste of her. I groan, wondering if I'll ever get enough of her as I inhale the scent of her shampoo. I ease into her, nuzzling into her neck and cupping her breast. A sleepy moan escapes her and she reaches her arm back, raking her fingers over my head.

"I'm gonna make things better for you, Siren. For you and Harlee," I promise, knowing that I mean every word. Neve turns her head slightly, pressing her lips against mine. I continue to move, slow and gentle, dragging out the warm feeling building between us. This doesn't feel like all the other times. We're not fucking. We're making love. And for me, that's a first.

Chapter Eight

Neve

I lie awake watching the sun rise. Ryder's words are running on loop through my mind. I've known him a little over a week and he's making promises of protecting me against Finn, the man who's ruined my life and continues to do so. I sigh heavily. Involving Ryder in my mess would be a huge mistake. There's already some kind of animosity between the pair and Finn's warned me to stay away from him. But I can't deny Ryder's words gave me some hope. The thought of having him around, makes me feel happier inside.

Ryder stirs beside me, instantly feeling around until his arm hooks around my waist. He pulls me against him and his erection pokes my thigh. I smile. *Does he ever get soft?* "Morning, Siren," he mumbles against my hair. "I could do with that coffee if the offer still stands?"

I sit, holding the sheet against my naked body while I look around for my clothes. Ryder reaches beside the bed and retrieves his own shirt, passing it to me. I smile to myself as I pull it over my head, inhaling his musky scent. When I stand, it almost comes to my knees.

Downstairs, I set up a tray, unsure of how Ryder takes his coffee, and load it with sugar, milk and two cups of black coffee. I head back upstairs and am about to go into the room when I notice Ryder is talking to someone. I pause, not meaning to listen in, but unable to stop myself because his hushed tone makes me suspicious.

"Brother, I can't send the video now, Finn was a complete dick to her, if he sees the recording of us fucking, then he'll take it out on their daughter. We need a new plan."

I stand frozen to the spot with a rush of emotions ripping through me. And somewhere in the back of my mind, I hear that negative voice telling me it was always too good to be true, who the hell was I kidding thinking this gorgeous biker was ever going to look at me, a run down, single mum, controlled by her abusive ex. I scoff to myself, shaking my head. I'm an idiot.

I take a deep breath before using my foot to push the door open wider and stepping into the room. Ryder immediately pulls the phone from his ear, disconnecting the call without saying goodbye.

"I wasn't sure how you took your coffee," I say with a forced smile as I lay the tray on the bed.

He stands, he's completely naked and not at all ashamed as he heads for the en-suite. "I need the bathroom," he says with a wink.

I glance at his mobile lying on the bed, still lit up and showing his home screen. I glance back to the bathroom where the door is now closed. I snatch the device up before I can change my mind and go straight for his gallery to check his videos. I notice the first video is recorded a few days ago and my thumb hovers over the play button. I need to see it for myself so I don't make a fool of myself. I press play. The video is shaky at first, and then the phone is placed on to something solid, pointing at an empty desk. I skip it forward until I come into view, with Ryder kissing me. I watch him push me against the desk, his mouth hungrily travelling over my body. I'm so mortified, I don't hear Ryder come back into the room right away, and when he clears his throat, I look up.

"There a reason you're looking through my phone?" He looks mildly irritated and I resist the urge to scream at him.

Instead, I place it back on the bed. "Is there a reason you have a video of us together in your office?"

His expression changes and for a brief second, I think he's panicking. He soon recovers, stepping closer. "It's not what you think," he begins and I roll my eyes. "It's not. Things have changed."

"That's not what I asked, Ryder. Why the fuck is there a video of me on your phone?"

He places his hands on his hips and bows his head while he thinks up his next line of bullshit. "I admit when I found out about you and Finn, I came up with a stupid plan to get him back. But now I-"

"Just go," I snap, unable to hear his plan. "We don't need to discuss it because it's pretty obvious, so please save me the humiliation and just leave."

"If you'll just let me explain," he begs.

I begin to grab his clothes, ripping off his t-shirt and adding it to the pile. "I don't need you to, Ryder. I get it, okay. Of course you're using me, it's obvious isn't it. I mean, why would you even look at me?" I say, my voice shaking with hurt.

"It's not like that."

"But it was," I yell, shoving his clothes to his chest and holding them there until he finally takes them. "It was exactly like that and I was an idiot to think otherwise."

"You're not an idiot," he mutters, beginning to dress. "If you'll just hear me out."

"I can't stop you sending that video to Finn," I say, grabbing my own shirt and pulling it on. "But know that he will take my daughter from me, and that will be on you. Whatever the deal is between the two of you, it isn't my fault."

"I won't send it to Finn. I'll delete it now." He grabs the phone and opens it up, showing me as he presses the delete button. "Until last night, I had every intention of sending it," he admits. "But now . . . well things have changed."

"Because I found out," I say, beginning to strip the sheets from my bed.

He tries to help but I yank them from his grip. "No," he argues, "Because last night was different between us and you know it was."

I shake my head, dumping the sheets in a pile on the floor. "It was just sex, Ryder. We hook up, that's what we do."

He balls his fists at his sides angrily. "Bullshit, Neve. You know it was different, you felt it as well as I did."

I glare at him, "I felt good, Ryder, you always make me feel good. But after, when reality hits, I realise you're just the same as every other man. Good for a fuck, and not much else. Now get the fuck out."

He heads for the door, turning back as I gather the bedding into my arms again. "I will be back, Neve," he says with promise. "You're not ready to hear me out and I get it, but you will listen to me eventually. And for the record, we're no longer just hooking up. I put you on the back of my bike and that might mean fuck all to you, but in my world, it's fucking huge. So, I'll be back and you will hear me out." He leaves, and my heart sinks when I hear the front door slam closed. I lower myself to sit on the bed, still clutching the dirty sheets and I burst into tears.

Sometime later, after I'd finally pulled myself together and Harlee was safely back in my care, I arranged to meet with Mya in our local coffee shop. If anyone can make me feel better, it's her.

I fill her in while we wait for our coffees. When the waitress places them in front of us, Mya adds three sugars to hers and stirs it. "He seemed so nice; I don't get why he'd do that."

"You know that stuff is addictive," I say, nodding to the sugar pot.

"So is sex, doesn't mean I'm giving it up anytime soon, it makes me happy."

"Speaking of giving it up, did you give it up to Griff?" I ask, arching a brow.

"Give what up Mummy?" Harlee asks, looking up from her colouring book. Mya smirks, watching me expectedly for my explanation.

"Her balloon Harl's, Griff wanted Aunt Mya's balloon," I say, without blinking. Harlee frowns and goes back to colouring.

"Mums are far too good at that, it scares me how much my mum might have done that to me," says Mya.

"You have to be a quick thinker in this game, or they'll smell your fear and take you down," I warn, adding a wink.

"No, seems Griff wasn't interested in my balloon after all, despite me offering to hand it right over. All a girl wants is a little balloon popping now and again, trust me to choose the only biker ever to not want the balloon," she continues, and I laugh out loud. "I've read the books yah know, meeting these guys, started something, and let me tell you, in the books he always takes the balloon."

"Well maybe just offering yourself like that scares him?" I suggest. "You are a bit full on when it comes to someone you like."

"Oh please, he's either gay or..." she trails off and shrugs, "Well just gay."

"Mya," I gasp, narrowing my eyes. "Just because he doesn't fancy you back, doesn't mean he's gay."

"I have never had a man turn me down," she hisses, "So I'm just saying that something must be wrong." I laugh, shaking my head in disbelief. "Anyway, I'm over it. I've set my sights on Knox, he's just as fit."

"Personally, I think you're crazy. I'm steering clear of them from this day forward," I say with confidence.

"Um, maybe you'll need to hold on to that thought because Ryder's just walked in."

My eyes widen. "What?" I hiss, not daring to look behind me.

"Oh shit, he's spotted us . . . he's coming over." She sits straighter and smiles past me. "Hey, Ryder. You don't seem the type to frequent a coffee shop."

"I didn't get my early morning caffeine hit so thought I'd stop by and grab one now," he replies, and I feel him standing behind me.

"Can I ask you something?" she adds and he must nod because she smiles. "Is Griff gay?" I groan, burying my head in my hands. "Because I have to tell you, I'm giving him all of the signals and he's just knocking me back."

He pulls out the seat beside Neve and lowers into it. I scowl at Mya and she mouths the word sorry. "Griff is very fussy when it comes to women," he says.

The waitress comes bounding over, her perky breasts practically hitting Ryder in the face as she smiles brightly at him. "What can I get you?" she asks.

Neve hides behind a menu, laughing and Ryder raises his eyebrows in her direction, moving his head back slightly to avoid headbutting the girl's chest. "Coffee, white, no sugar, please," he tells her, with an awkward smile. He frowns as she bounds back to the counter, swaying her arse extra hard. He shakes his head in annoyance, I imagine he gets that kind of attention a lot.

"So, who are targeting today?" I ask, casually, "I have a camcorder if you'd like to borrow it. The quality is so much better than using your phone."

He sighs heavily, letting me know he's sick of my bullshit. "Hey Harlee, you're looking pretty today. You know you share your name with my motorbike?"

Harlee drags her attention away from her colouring to smile at him. "I like bikes," she says.

"If your mummy says it's okay, I can show you mine. It's right outside."

Harlee looks to me with wide, hopeful, eyes. I reluctantly nod, wondering if Ryder realises he's using my daughter to get to me, just like her father does. She squeals in delight and Ryder takes her tiny hand in his, leading her outside to where his bike is parked.

We watch for a few minutes through the window before Mya says, "You've got to admit, he looks pretty hot with a kid." I roll my eyes, even though deep down, I agree. Ryder carefully lifts Harlee onto the bike, keeping his hands on her waist to stop her slipping as she reaches forward to grip the handlebars. She's so excited, and I can see she's chatting his head off. It's nice to see after she came home so sad this morning. She refused to kiss Finn goodbye, and when I asked her about the incident the night before, she refused to speak about it, opting to distract me with questions about the stars and other random stuff.

"Maybe I should just hear him out?" I say, thinking out loud. Mya smirks and I narrow my eyes. "It doesn't mean anything. I just think he's gonna keep hassling me until I do."

She holds her hands up defensively. "I wasn't thinking anything, but you're right, he's not going to give up, and it can't hurt to listen. I'll take Harlee back to mine. If you talk here, it can't get heated."

I nod in agreement and she gathers her things, along with Harlee's. She swoops down to kiss my cheek, "Goodluck." And then she steps out to where Ryder is lifting Harlee from his bike. They exchange words and she leaves with Harlee. Ryder steps back inside, he doesn't look so confident now as he takes a seat opposite me. "Mya said you're ready to talk?"

I nod. "I figured you'd keep turning up where I am until I agreed to listen to your bullshit."

"I can't even begin to tell you how sorry I am," he begins and I sigh, arching a brow.

"I don't want to hear how sorry you are, Ryder. Why the hell did you do it?"

He places his hands on the table, linking his fingers and staring down at them for a moment. "I'm finding life hard right now," he admits, "Since coming out of the nick, everything feels chaotic and overwhelming." I like that he's finally giving me real talk, so I remain quiet while he continues. "My brother's look up to me, they expect me to lead like I did all those years ago, but I've changed. I'm not the same as I was."

"In what way?"

He shrugs, looking uncomfortable and I sense he doesn't often talk openly about his feelings. "I shouldn't have made you a target, Neve. It was stupid and fucked up. The first night I met you, when you came over and talked non-stop, you woke something inside of me." He gives a small smile. "And I thought you were going to be a one-night stand. But after, I couldn't stop thinking about you. That's never happened to me before. When I found out about Finn, I thought I'd kill two birds with one stone. I thought I just needed to fuck you out my system and if there was a way to get one over on Finn too, well, that was a bonus. It was stupid," he explains. "I know that now. But honestly, the thought of seeing you again was the main reason. I told myself it was part of some plan, to appease the voice inside that was questioning why the fuck I needed to see you again. That's not something I've even done." He pauses, "It scares me."

"Why?" I ask.

"Because I'm not used to these feelings you evoke inside me, Neve. The thought of losing you makes me sick to my stomach. I can't not see you again."

I frown. I want to believe him, I do. But it's only been a short time and even though I know how he feels, because I feel it too, I don't trust him. "What did Finn do to you?" I ask, changing the subject.

"He set me up. I can't let that go."

"Set you up how?"

"I don't wanna talk about Finn right now," he says firmly, and I sense that's final. "But he crossed me, taking my freedom. I can't let that lie, Neve. He has to pay or it'll not only eat me up inside, but I'll lose the respect of the club, and I can't be a president with no respect."

I already know that respect is important to him so I nod. "Okay. But where does that leave me?"

"That depends on what you want from me," he says.

My heart leaps a little. The fact he's giving me a choice shows he's respecting my feelings. And I want to tell him all the things I'm thinking, that the romantic in me wants the whole thing, marriage, kids, forever. I almost smile to myself. There's clearly a bunny boiler inside of me but I don't want to scare him away so I shrug, "What do you want?"

He laughs. "You're gonna throw it back at me to test the waters?" he asks, and I nod again. He reaches over the table and takes my hands in his. That move alone makes my heart leap. "I want it all," he says firmly, looking me in the eye. I swallow hard. "I want you. I want forever."

"And Harlee?" I whisper, mesmerised by the seriousness in his tone.

"She's part of you, right. It's not even a question."

"It's a lot. Taking on someone else's child, especially when you hate her father. It's so complicated," I say.

"Only if you let it be, Neve. After hearing that prick last night and the way he hit her, fuck, I wanted to rip his head off and I hadn't even met Harlee. Now I have, that urge is even worse."

Chapter Nine

Ryder

She's hesitant, I can see it in her eyes. "You've got every reason not to trust me," I tell her. "But give me a chance to prove I like you."

"You're offering me a fairy tale," she says quietly. "You're going to be my knight in shining armour to rescue me and my baby girl." I nod. She slowly pulls her hands from my grasp and places them in her lap and my heart sinks. "But fairy tales aren't real, Ryder. There is no knight and the only real part, is the big bad wolf waiting to ruin my life. He's real. Finn will never allow me to be with you, of all people."

"Finn doesn't get a say," I snap. The fear she's pulling away scares the shit out of me and that's how I know this is real. "I feel more for you in a couple of weeks, than I've ever felt for anyone. I know I sound crazy, and if my brothers could hear me now, they'd think I've lost my mind. But I've wasted years of my life and I won't waste anymore waiting for the right moment. I know how I feel about you. Just take a chance, Neve."

"And when Finn starts kicking off?"

"I'll handle it."

"How?"

"Does it matter?" I can't tell her the level of violence I feel when I see that prick, so I'll be welcoming the day he kicks off, just so I can lay into him.

"He'll take Harlee from me," she mutters, her words laced with worry.

"That's not going to happen, Siren. I won't let it. Just say you'll give me a chance and I will protect you from him."

"You can't," she whispers.

"I can. I promise. There'll be no more phone calls with him checking on you, no more threats to take Harlee away. Agree to be mine and that all stops."

"Yours?" she repeats, almost looking amused. "What does that even mean?"

"It means you become my ol' lady," the words tumble out before I've thought them through, but they feel right. "And I protect you with my life, and so do my club."

"Just a few hours ago, I found out you were using me to get to Finn. Now you're basically telling me you want to look after me and spend forever with me?" she asks, arching a brow. "You don't even know me."

"I know enough to know we deserve a chance to explore whatever's going on between us. You must feel it too, Neve. We've got something." She bites on her lower lip and I know I've got her so I smile, reaching over the table to tug her lip free. "Yes?" She gives a nod, a small smile playing on her lips.

I stand, pulling her with me and wrapping my arms around her. I kiss her hard, lifting her off her feet. "Thank you," I whisper against her lips. "You won't regret it."

I'd dropped Neve off at Mya's with the promise to call by later. And now, sitting at my desk in my office, I can't help the permanent smile on my face. I'll give it some time before I announce to the club I've taken an ol' lady. I don't want to scare Neve off completely, but I can't fucking wait to have her here with me.

A knock at the door breaks my daydreaming and Griff comes in looking pissed. The last few days he's had a frown fixed on his face but we're not the sort to talk feelings. Or at least we weren't before I got sent down. We've never been like that, even though we're close and have always been since the day he was born. I take a deep breath before asking, "You okay?"

He frowns, looking at me like I've lost my mind before muttering, "Yeah, you?"

"I'm good," I say, "Me and Neve are working things out." I'd told him about the fact she'd discovered my plan.

He looks surprised. "I didn't see that coming, she always seems so hard faced. How did you manage to convince her you're not a total dick head?"

I snigger. "Because I'm not." He scoffs and I laugh. "I like her, Griff," I say more seriously. "When I'm with her, the world makes sense. My heads been fucked for so long and she calms the crazy. I haven't felt like that since . . ." I trail off and Griff gives a sympathetic smile.

"What about Finn?"

I smirk. "Finn is going to get what's coming to him. Did you know he makes Neve call him every night to make sure she's alone?"

Griff shudders, "The bloke gives me the creeps. When I first saw him with her, I didn't like the way he was with her, like she's his property. And the kid looks terrified of him."

"Yeah well, I'd be lying if I said I wasn't looking forward to him finding out about the two of us," I admit. "I've agreed to let her do it in her own time, she's shit scared of him. But I have a feeling he'll know sooner rather than later. I'm not a patient man when it comes to claiming what's mine."

Griff laughs. "Careful Pres, that sounds a bit like you're laying claim." I arch a brow and he sits straighter. "You're fucking laying claim?"

So much for me keeping it to myself. "Like I said, I'm impatient."

Neve

Work is hell. It's chaotic and this is the fifth complaint I've had to deal with in less than an hour. I wave to get the porters attention and he rushes over. "Can you go to the holding rooms and see if you can find a bag belonging to Mr Hart, it hasn't arrived in his room yet." He gives a nod and rushes off. I turn back to the angry customer. "I apologise again, Mr. Hart. Please go to your room and someone will bring your luggage right up."

I've been working at the Hotel Le Pruzé for the last two years and I love it. I can fit my shifts around Harlee's nursery and my boss is pretty relaxed. But as I step out into the busy London street after my busy three-hour shift, I sigh in relief. All I've thought about all day is getting home to snuggle with Harlee. And the fact Ryder is calling around later tonight is also putting a spring in my step.

"We need to talk." Finn steps in my path, halting me. My heart drops like it always does when I see him. When I spoke with Ryder on the phone last night, I'd agreed to try and be stronger around Finn and not let him push me around so much, but it's easier said than done when he just turns up like this and I'm unprepared.

"I have to get back for Harlee," I say, coldly. "I get charged extra if I run over her time slot with the childminder."

"Call her, I'll pay the extra," he says firmly.

There's not point arguing with him when he's got a steely look of determination on his face so I pull out my mobile and send Mya a quick text telling her I'm running late. I've never had a childminder for Harlee, which just shows how much he takes notice of where his daughter is. When I have an afternoon shift, one of the girls usually grabs Harlee from nursery for me.

He gets out his wallet and pulls out two fresh twenties, handing them to me. "My office," he adds, walking ahead.

I reluctantly follow with a heavy heart. We go into the large building and his receptionist automatically stands the second she sees Finn. I always thought she did this out of respect, but looking at her face now, I think it might be fear. I give her a sympathetic smile as he completely ignores her and goes into his office.

He waits for me to step in before slamming the door and locking it. For a second, I panic, wondering if Ryder's told Finn about us but as he closes the blinds to the window looking out over the open plan office, he says. "Harlee told someone at school I hit her."

I stare open mouthed. Harlee refused to speak to me about it, but she's told someone else. "Who did she tell?"

"Her teaching assistant."

"Okay, well what did you say?" I ask, my heart hammering in my chest.

"I said that she was lying," he snaps, "What was I supposed to say?"

I gasp. "The truth," I screech. "You should have told the truth. Now they'll question us all and it'll look suspicious," I yell angrily.

I don't see his hand until it connects with my cheek and I fall back, hitting the wall. Pain shoots through my shoulder and my cheek burns. I grasp it, wincing as I try hard to blink away the tears that threaten to fall. It's been a long time since Finn's hit me and I can't say I've missed it. "I'm not a fucking idiot," he spits angrily. "Don't talk to me like I am," he warns. I wait for him to move out my face before taking a calming breath. Finn paces. "You need to tell them she's lying. Say she's been doing that a lot lately for attention or some shit."

"No. They'll know that's not true."

"How?" he bellows and I flinch. "You're her mother, they'll listen to you."

"They'll have already questioned her, Finn," I say firmly. "They'll have written everything down. You have to tell them the truth."

"Say someone else did it," he says with a shrug. "I don't know, tell them your biker friends did it."

I stare in disbelief. "I can't do that, Finn. I can't lie."

"You'll lie or I'll make your life hell," he warns, sneering.

I scoff. "You already do, Finn."

He moves close again and I turn my head to one side to avoid the feel of his warm breath on me. He runs a finger down my arm. "I miss you," he whispers, "And it's been a while since we fucked," he adds. I shiver with repulsion. "Don't make me do it in anger, baby, you know that hurts us both."

"I'll sort it," I whisper, my voice shaking in fear.

"Sorry?" he asks, and I can feel the smirk coming from him.

"I said I'll sort it with the school," I say a little louder.

He steps closer until his body is pressed against mine and I flinch, pressing myself as hard against the wall as I can just to try and put an inch between us. "Good girl," he whispers, pressing his nose into my hair and inhaling. "I knew you'd see sense." He steps back and I sag in relief. "Now run along and sort this mess out. Call me when it's done."

The second I step outside, tears roll down my cheeks. I swipe at them angrily. He doesn't deserve anymore tears of mine. I pull out my mobile and call the school, asking to speak with Harlee's teacher. She's a wonderful teacher and Harlee adores her, she reminds me of Miss Honey from Matilda and when her softly spoken voices fill the line, I can't help but smile.

"Hi, I just spoke with Harlee's father and he said she'd told the teaching assistant he hit her?" I push my way into the busy street, heading for home.

"Yes, that's correct. We were very surprised when he told us she was lying."

"I think it was a misunderstanding," I explain. "They were play fighting and he did tap her on the leg but it wasn't hard and by no means a punishment."

"Harlee was pretty clear that it hurt."

I give a laugh. "I know, she came right to me after it happened and said the same but I was there," I lie, "And it really was a playful tap. I think she was being a little dramatic. She's finding our split hard."

"I understand. Thank you for clearing it up."

I disconnect the call and sigh with relief. Then I send a text to Finn telling him I've sorted it.

By the time I get home, I've managed to compose myself. "Hi hunny, I'm home," I call out to Mya as I make my way through to the kitchen and grab a pack of ice, pressing it to my cheek.

"Are you okay?" she calls back.

I go into the living room where she's sitting with Harlee watching television. I lean against the door frame and force a smile. "All good. You?"

She watches me with suspicious eyes. "That his handy work?" she asks, giving me a pointed stare.

"I'm fine," I mutter. I lean over the back of the couch and kiss Harlee on the head. "How was your day, Popple?" I ask.

"Good," she says on a yawn.

The doorbell rings out and I glance at Mya nervously. If Finn's here, I can't deal with him and as if she reads my mind, she gets up to answer it. A minute later she calls to me, "It's Ryder."

My heart does a happy leap and I go through to the hall, "Then let him in," I tell her and she steps to one side.

Ryder's eyes fix on the ice pack and he immediately tugs my hand away to check. "What happened?"

I shrug, "I fell, stupid really," I lie.

Mya closes the door, "I'll watch Harlee," she mutters going into the living room and closing the door.

"I stopped by the hotel to give you a ride home," he says, following me through to the kitchen. I wince, keeping my back to him as my mind races to think up another lie. "And imagine my surprise when the guy on the desk told me you left with Finn."

I turn to face him, "Sorry. I didn't say because I didn't want to argue about it."

He moves closer until I'm pressed against the counter and his body his flanking mine. "And this," he asks, gently rubbing a thumb over my cheek.

"Harlee told the nursery that Finn hit her," I say, trying to distract him. "I had to call them and sort it out . . ."

"The mark on your skin, Neve," he says, more firmly.

"And things got heated between us because he was stressed and . . ."

Ryder pushes off the counter with a deadly look in his eye, and heads for the door. I rush after him, grabbing his arm frantically, "No, don't go to him," I beg. "Please, you'll make it worse."

He shrugs me off and my bruised shoulder hits the wall again, this time I cry out, gripping it. Ryder frowns, taken my wrist in his hand and holding me still while he lifts the sleeve of my shirt. There's a deep bruise forming and he arches a brow, waiting for me to speak. "Please," I whisper, tears springing to my eyes. "Don't go there and cause an issue."

He sighs, pulling me against his chest and holding me. "Siren, this can't go on. He put his fucking hands on you. I can't let that slide. What did you tell the school?"

"I lied," I admit, feeling shame wash over me. "I said it was play fighting."

"Jesus. And what happens when he does it again?"

I cry harder. "I know, okay, but I was scared and I didn't know what else to do."

"You have me now, Neve. Next time, you call me. Next time, you don't go anywhere with him alone. Next time, I'll make sure I'm there to make shit clear. That man stays the fuck away from you and if he lays a hand on you or Harlee again, I'll cut them off." He presses his lips to mine and walks me back to the kitchen. "Tomorrow we go to the school and speak to the head teacher. She needs to know the situation."

I shake my head. "She hates me, she's a witch."

I grin. "I know her well, trust me, she'll listen."

I frown, wondering how someone like him could know someone like Miss Hind. She's a stuck-up cow and I can't think of any situation that would mean her and Ryder are friends.

Chapter Ten

Ryder

Neve grips my hand tightly as we sit outside the head teacher's office. It took me a while to convince her that she needed to be honest about her situation with Finn because she needed a record of the shit he's been doing, in case he does try and take Harlee.

The door swings open and Sissy, or Sarah as she's known to others, pops her head out. Her smile freezes the second she lays her eyes on me and her expression changes to one of shock. I stand, pulling Neve with me. "Hey Sassy," I say with a smile. "Long time."

"Ryder," she murmurs to herself, like she can't quite believe her eyes. She's just how I remember her, only sterner looking. Her red hair is pinned up in a tight bun and her green eyes aren't as bright as they used to be.

She steps to one side and we go into the office. She points to the two vacant seats and we sit. She goes around to her side and lowers graciously into her seat. "What can I do for you?" she asks, not making eye contact with me. A part of me thought she'd be happier to see me, but right now she looks annoyed.

"It's about what Harlee told the teacher yesterday," says Neve.

Sassy opens a paper file. "About her father hitting her?"

"Yes."

"I thought this was cleared up last night?" she asks, fixing Neve with a stern glare.

"I lied," says Neve and Sassy frowns. "I was scared and Finn made me call and lie."

"Miss Lawerance, are you saying it wasn't exaggerated?" Her tone is clipped and Neve reddens with embarrassment.

"Come on Sass," I mutter, "It was hard for her to come here today and say all this," I tell her.

She finally brings her eyes to me. "My name is Miss Hind." I feel the frostiness and smirk. "What is your relation to the child exactly, Ethan?" she adds, quirking a brow.

I sigh and feel Neve's eyes on me. I hadn't told her my real name, until this moment I hadn't thought to. No one uses it but Sassy. "I'm here to support Neve."

"What a good Samaritan," she mutters, her voice dripping with sarcasm. "So, Mrs Lawerence. Are you telling me Harlee wasn't lying and her father did in fact hit her?"

Neve nods, "Yes. I have spoken to him and told him he's not allowed to do that again."

"Does it happen often?"

Neve shakes her head. "No. That was the first time."

"That he struck Harlee," I add in, and Neve lets go of my hand. "You have to be honest," I remind her.

"Should I be concerned that Harlee is in danger?" Sarah asks.

"No," I confirm. "Not anymore."

"She sees her father at the weekends, but I think this has taught him a lesson, he won't hit her again," says Neve.

"Because he won't be having contact alone," I add.

Neves eyes burn into the side of my head. We hadn't discussed it but it's a sensible move. He can't be trusted with her alone. "And you're getting a court order on that, are you?" Sassy asks, making notes in the file.

"It'll be enforced," I confirm and Sassy sighs, looking up to me again.

"By law?" she repeats.

I smirk. "You know how this works, Sass," I say, winking.

She doesn't appreciate it and instead, lays her pen down. "No, I don't. Please explain."

"Look, we can do this, Sassy, we can. I will listen while you yell at me and list all the reasons you hate my guts. But let's not do it right now."

"In front of your new girlfriend?" she asks.

I didn't expect this to be an issue, I'd heard she'd moved on and was now happy with some banking guy. "We're here to talk about Harlee."

"I can leave," says Neve, standing.

"No, you don't need to," I say, groaning at the shit show this is turning into. "Come on, Sassy, I thought I could rely on you to be professional here."

It's a low blow and she scoffs angrily. "Fuck you, Ethan." Neve walks to the door and before I can protest, Sassy adds, "When were you going to tell me you were out?"

"I'm here, telling you," I snap. "Neve, wait . . ." I add.

"Don't you think I deserve a little more respect than you showing up to my office with your new bit of arse?"

Neve leaves, closing the door hard behind her. "Great," I mutter. "Thanks for that."

"What did you expect, a welcoming hug?" Sassy snaps.

"Yes, actually. Haven't you moved on?" I snap. "Isn't that what your last letter said?"

"You refused to see me," she yells angrily. "Was I supposed to just sit around waiting?"

"Yes," I growl. "Yes because you were my ol' lady and that's what you were supposed to do."

She takes a calming breath, staring down at her hands. "Yeah well, I got tired of waiting."

"I'd appreciate you pulling some strings with the whole Harlee situation," I mutter.

"I'm sure you would but I don't do shit like that now, Ethan. I'm all above board and this is a safeguarding issue."

"I'm taking care of it. He won't be alone with the kid again, I promise."

She eyes me for a second. "Fine. I'll note what you've told me today for the record, but you have to make sure he isn't allowed to be alone with her again, even if that means taking him to court. Okay?"

I nod. "I appreciate it."

Neve

I don't bother to wait for Ryder. I'm angry and I don't even know why. Maybe I feel humiliated or maybe I just feel embarrassed. Why didn't he warn me he had a connection to Miss Hind. A deep connection. If she was his ol' lady, they were practically married, and in the eyes of the club, they were married. It just highlights all the things I still don't know about him. Like his fucking name. Why did I assume he was called Ryder? And why didn't he tell me otherwise? I growl out loud and a few passer-by, glance my way warily.

By the time I get home, Ryder is waiting for me outside. I ignore him and unlock the front door, he follows me in. "Well that was a shit show," I snap, tugging my coat off and throwing it on the side.

"You shouldn't have walked home alone. You should have waited outside."

"That's all you have to say?" I yell. "You take me to meet your ol' lady and all you care about is me walking home without you?"

"She's not my ol' lady."

"But she was, right, at some point she was."

"Before I got sent down," he says. "And I misjudged how much she hates me, I thought she'd be happier."

I scoff, "Then it's clearly been a while since you last saw her because she's always like that. A cold, sour faced bitch."

Ryder laughs, "You don't like her?"

"Nobody likes her, *Ethan*," I say, arching a brow when I say his real name.

"I should have told you, I didn't think."

"Yah know what, I just need a minute," I say, pinching the bridge of my nose. "To process."

He moves closer, taking my hand and gently tugging me to him. "I'm sorry I didn't warn you and I'm sorry I didn't tell you my real name."

"You said Finn wasn't going to see Harlee alone again," I mutter.

"Do you really want him alone with her?"

"Of course not, but I don't get to decide that, Ryder. He's her dad, I can't just cut him out."

"He hit her. The school are taking it seriously. Sassy-"

"Miss Hind," I cut in childishly.

"Miss Hind," he corrects, "Is letting it rest on file but if he does anything else like this, it'll go to safeguarding."

"You should go," I mutter.

"Don't be mad over this, Neve," he says, sighing. "I'm trying to take care of you both."

"I'm her mother and I make those decisions, Ryder, or Ethan or whatever the fuck people call you," I snap. "Just give me some time to think it over."

He mutters something to himself, before storming out.

Ryder

She's upset, and I get it. But I promised to keep her and Harlee safe and I don't see why she's putting up a fight. I head over to Griff's, I want to keep an eye on Neve's place in case Finn should turn up unannounced.

I try the front door but it's locked. "Fuck sake," I mutter in irritation. Griff's bike is parked up on the driveway so I know he's here. I knock and wait for a few minutes but he doesn't answer so I head around the back. I've asked for a key numerous times, but he refuses to give me one. He likes his privacy which is the reason he decided to rent this place when I got out of prison. He'd spent the last few years as acting president and when I got out he told me he was renting his own space for a few months, being around the men twenty-four-seven had driven him mad. Personally, I like it at the club.

I try the back door and it opens, much to my relief. I head in, but he's not downstairs which makes me think he's probably balls deep in pussy. I grin to myself as I head up the stairs. I need a piss anyway, and I need to know if Mya is in his bed, wondering if her charms had finally paid off.

I stop outside his room to the sound of groans and laugh to myself as I kick the door open. "Taking the afternoon off . . ." I stare at the scene before me, my words hanging in the air.

Griff scrambles to grab a sheet but it's far too late to hide the fact he's fucking another guy. "Fuck, Ryder, how did you get in?" he snaps, wrapping the sheet around himself.

The man on the bed flops onto his back, his semi hard cock fully on show. "Hey, I'm Corey," he says with a small wave.

I glance at Griff for an explanation but he's staring at the ground. "Eric?" I almost whisper. The word feels tight in my throat but it gets his attention, probably because I never use it. "What the fucks going on?"

"I'm sorry," he mutters.

"Sorry?" I repeat. "I don't understand . . . you . . ." I glance back at Corey. "But you like . . . you're not . . ."

"I'm sorry you had to find out like this," mutters Griff.

"Find out what, Griff?" I snap. "Is this just fun or are you . . ."

"I am," he confirms.

I grip the doorframe, hardly believing what I just walked in on. My mind races trying to remember a time when Griff was with a woman. "You're what?" I ask, needing to hear the words.

"Ryder, please," he mumbles.

"Say the fucking words, Griff," I yell and he jumps at my tone.

"I'm gay," he grits the words out angrily. "I'm fucking gay."

I inhale sharply at his confession. I hadn't even suspected. I turn and leave, rushing back down the stairs with Griff yelling for me to wait and talk.

I break out into the fresh air and jump on my bike. I need space. From my brother. From my club and from Neve.

Neve

It's been almost a week since I asked Ryder to leave. Almost a week since I last saw him and almost a week since I last spoke with him. He's ignored my calls and the two text messages I've sent asking if he's okay. And now I'm officially worried, so I knock on Griff's door for answers.

He opens it and I take a step back. He's looking pale and tired. There are dark circles under his eyes and he's missing that annoying grin that's always plastered on his face. "I just wanted to check if everything was okay because I haven't heard from Ryder since Tuesday and it's now the weekend and he hasn't answered my calls." I feel my cheeks redden with embarrassment. I feel like a desperate idiot now I've said the words out loud.

He opens the door wider without a word and heads back inside. I follow to the kitchen where a topless blond guy is sitting drinking coffee and reading the newspaper. He doesn't look like a biker, and I haven't seen him with the guys before and when he looks up to see me, he smiles, only confirming my suspicions because the guys never smile . . . apart from Griff.

"Corey meet my neighbour, Neve," Griff mutters, sitting down at the table. He points to an empty chair and I sit too. "Ryder ain't mad at you," he adds, taking Corey's coffee and sipping it.

"We argued on Tuesday, I asked him to give me space," I confess.

"He's hit the road," he explains.

"What does that mean?"

"It means he's off radar."

"Until when?" I ask, wondering if he does this sort of thing regular.

Griff shrugs and then taking pity on me he adds, "It's not you he's running from. It's me. He found something out and this is his way of dealing with it."

"Or not," mutters Corey.

"So you've spoken to him?" I ask.

"No. He text me to say he's taking some time out."

I push down the hurt feeling his words cause me. The fact he's not even answered me, when I clearly pointed out I was worried, pisses me off. "Well, at least he's okay. Sorry to have bothered you," I say, rising to my feet.

"Why did you argue?" Griff asks.

"I met his ex, Sassy," I tell him.

He gives low whistle, "She's a cold bitch."

I nod in agreement. "I was jealous," I admit, "and I told him I needed space to clear my head. Stupid really," I mutter. Ryder was only trying to help but I was so pissed about the whole Sassy thing, I overreacted. "What did he find out about?" I ask.

Griff gives a small unamused laugh. "He caught me fucking Corey."

I stare back and forth between the pair, waiting for one of them to laugh like it's a joke but when they don't, I say, "Mya will be so relieved, she thought it was her."

Griff laughs, "I told her not to take it personally. If I was into women, she'd be first on my list."

"So Ryder just took off?" I ask, and the pain returns to Griff's face.

"I should have told him. There was no reason not to. The other guys in the club know. But with Ryder being inside, I just never found the right time to tell him. I even took this house so he wouldn't find out." He groans rubbing his tired face. "I fucked up. He hates secrets." He stands as I head for the door. "Look, I'll text him and tell him to call you. It's not fair for him to ghost you like this."

I open the front door, "God no, please don't do that. I don't want the pity text. Look Harlee is at her father's tonight. Why don't we get together and have a few drinks. There's no reason we can't get along just because your brother is an arse," I suggest. Griff looks like he needs a friend right now, one without balls and tattoos.

Griff nods. "I'd like that, Siren. Consider it a date."

Chapter Eleven

Ryder

I stop my bike on the roadside and stare at the bar where Neve is inside. I track her phone. Not that she's aware, but I needed to know she was safe from that prick, Finn. And when shit gets real, he's going to up his games and I have to be prepared.

I've spent the last few days just riding and fuck it's felt good. I've missed the road and if I didn't have Neve back here waiting for me, I'd consider doing that shit permanently. But it worked, it cleared my mind and now I know I want her more than anything.

I watch as my brother lifts Neve onto a table and they begin to sing a bad version of Meatloaf's 'I'll do anything for love, but I won't do that.' They're yelling more than singing and it's loud enough for me to hear from over the street.

Griff joins her on the table and I spot Corey watching. My heart twists. I hate he couldn't come to me and be honest about his sexuality. I'd never look at him any differently, he's my little brother and I love him.

I light another cigarette, inhaling deeply and closing my eyes. I'll never sort this shit out if I stand out here watching them, so I head towards the bar. As I get closer, I spot Neve disappearing through a side door. I frown, looking to the side of the building just as a fire exit door swings open, and Neve tumbles out giggling, hand in hand with a guy.

I wait in the shadows, my fist clenched and my jaw tight. The guy kicks the door shut and pushes Neve against it. She's giggling again and the sound irritates me. "Now you have me all alone, what will you do with me?" she asks in a breathless voice.

The man gently brushes her hair from her face and angles his face like he's going in for a kiss. I step from the shadows, dropping my cigarette to the ground and crushing it under my boot. I lean against the wall and sigh heavily. "It ain't even been a full week, Siren," I say.

The guy spins around, keeping Neve behind him. "What the fuck, man?" he demands.

I arch a brow. "Do you want your new friend to die in this dirty alleyway, Siren?" I ask, keeping my tone bored.

She steps out from behind the man, folding her arms over her chest. "What are you doing here, Ryder?"

"Surprise honey, I'm home," I say, smirking.

"Your timing is shit," she mutters.

"As is your choice in men tonight."

"You left, Ryder. What am I supposed to do, wait around in case you decide to show up? One minute you're promising me forever and the next you're gone. You ghosted me."

"I thought we were clear where we stood, Neve," I say, firmly. "I needed some time away."

"Well good for you but in case you haven't noticed, I'm busy."

"You heard the woman," the man chips in, "She doesn't want you here."

"You sure about that, Siren?" I ask, arching a brow. "You sure you want me to leave . . . forever?" She presses her lips together in a fine line and I see her wavering. "Or we can go back to your place. Talk?"

Neve turns to the man. "Sorry, I have to deal with this. Maybe another time?"

The man rolls his eyes, storming past me. I wink, slapping him on the back as he passes. "I didn't think you were the type of girl to be in dark alleyways with strangers," I say, stepping closer to her.

"We met in a cupboard, you fucked me," she says dryly.

I back her against the wall and place my hands above her head, caging her in. I lower my face until our lips are inches apart. "I'm so fucking jealous right now, I want to go after that prick and beat his face to a pulp just for being close to you." She inhales sharply. "It doesn't matter where I go, or how far, we are always together. Don't ever question that. Don't pull this shit again, the next guy won't walk away."

Neve

He's possessive and I like it. I shouldn't, not after everything with Finn, but this feels different with Ryder. I want him to own me, to possess me. He's watching me, staring hard into my eyes while his entire body cages me against the wall. With Ryder, I feel safe.

"You left," I whisper, the hurt still evident in my voice.

"Not you, Siren. I didn't leave you."

"I had to let Harlee go with Finn, you weren't there to stop it."

"I know," he says, "I was watching."

"The you saw how she cried and clung to me." He nods. "Why didn't you call me? Why didn't you answer my messages?" I hate how desperate I sound.

"You haven't told him about us, Siren."

"Because I thought you'd left."

He hooks a finger under my chin and tilts my head back. "I need to be inside you."

I'm under his spell, captivate by his dirty mouth, even though I swore to myself I wouldn't let him do this without explaining himself to me first. "We need to talk," I manage to say.

"After," he says, pushing off the wall and grabbing my hand.

I groan from exhaustion as Ryder pushes into me for the third time since we got home. "Ryder," I whisper, trying to guide his mouth away from my nipple. "You promised we'd talk."

"Anything you want, Siren," he whispers, sliding deeper into me until I arch my back.

"I want to know about Sassy," I say.

He sighs, climbing from me and lying beside me. I feel the loss immediately but he wraps his arm around me and pulls me into his side. "That's a real mood changer," he says with a laugh.

"Sorry."

"What do you want to know exactly?"

"How you met, she doesn't seem your type."

He laughs again. "Believe it or not, she's not the frosty bitch she makes out she is. I met her when we were both in our twenties. She was in some rich bitch bar and I was passing. She caught my eye and I walked right up to her and kissed her. She fell for my charm."

I run my finger over his tattoos, tracing a dragon. "Why did you break up?"

"I cheated on her," he admits and I glance up. "I'm not proud," he adds.

"So you met her, swept her off her feet and then cheated?"

"What can I say, I'm a prick. Or at least I was back then."

His fingers gently stroke my back and I feel my eyes growing heavy but I can't sleep when he's finally opening up. "How old are you?" I ask.

"Thirty-eight."

"You're eight years older than me," I tell him. "How old were you when you met Sassy?"

"I was twenty-eight and she twenty-four."

"Did you leave her for the other woman?"

"No. She caught me."

"Wow, no wonder she hates you. Did she know her?"

"I'm gonna be completely honest now, Neve," he says and his tone is suddenly serious. I sit up and turn to face him. He remains on his back, staring up at the ceiling. "I was cheating on Sassy with her sister."

It's not what I expected and my expression must show it because he also sits up and grabs my hand. "I want you to know I'm not the same man I was back then. I'd never do that to you."

"I need you to tell me everything, Ryder, right now," I demand.

He gives a nod. "There's no excuse for what I did. Alice was a year younger than Sass and she was jealous of her. I'm not making excuses, you can ask Sassy and she'll tell you it was always like that between them. Whatever Sassy had, Alice wanted. I was weak and a fucking idiot and when she came on to me, I encouraged it. We ended up having a cheap affair behind Sassy's back. She walked in on us and shit got ugly. They fought and I had to drag Sassy out of there. Alice was upset, she saw it as me choosing Sassy over her. By the time I'd got back to Alice, she'd worked herself up into a temper. We argued, like this huge volcano erupting, and it spilt out into the street. She ran. It turns out she was seeing a guy, he wasn't a good person and when he saw how upset she was over me, he got angry. I turned up there after he'd laid into her . . ." he pauses to compose himself. "She was clinging onto his arm, begging him . . ." he frowns, like he's lost in that memory. "Don't leave me. Don't leave me." He shudders. "And then he shoved her really hard and she stumbled back. Her head bounced of the kerb, Neve, I still hear that thud in my nightmares."

"Shit, what happened to her?"

"She died," he mutters and I gasp. "In my arms."

"What happened to the man?"

He shrugs. "He ran. The police showed up and I was cradling her body apparently telling her over and over I was sorry. With the neighbours seeing our fight, it looked like I'd killed her."

"Didn't they find the other guy?"

"They didn't care, Neve. I'm a fucking biker, they were just happy to put me away and they didn't give a crap if I was innocent or not. They got your ex, a bent lawyer, to screw me over for assault."

"Does Sassy know the truth?"

He nods. "Yeah, she knows I'm not like that. She believed me right from the start but I'd hurt her and she couldn't forgive me. I get it. That's not all," he says, glancing nervously at her. "I have a kid . . . with Sassy."

"Oh my god," I gasp, my hands covering my mouth. "How could you not tell me about that?"

"He's four and Sassy doesn't want me to have contact. He's settled and happy."

"Wait, you haven't even met him?"

He shakes his head and his shoulders hunch. "No. She wrote to me in prison and told me she'd met someone new soon after Alfie was born. As far as the kid knows, that's his dad. I can't rock up and ruin his world. It's selfish. He's doing great, Sassy has him in a private school and he's top of his class. It's the least I owe her after what I did."

"Oh, Ryder," I murmur, climbing onto his lap and wrapping myself around him. "That's got to be so hard."

"I'm good with her decision. I have no regrets there."

"You're a good man, Ryder and you'd be the perfect dad."

He gives a small smile. "Maybe one day I'll get a second chance."

I watch Neve pacing back and forth in front of the living room window. Finn was supposed to return Harlee at eleven, and now at half past twelve, there is still no sign.

"It's because I didn't answer his calls," she mutters.

"He'll bring her back," I say firmly, because if he doesn't, I'll be going to collect her myself.

I know the second he pulls up because Neve breathes a sigh of relief and rushes outside. I wait ten seconds, counting each one carefully before following Neve. I stand in the doorway, leaning against the frame and watching as Finn kisses Neve on the head. She turns away slightly, making it obvious she's uncomfortable. He opens the back door and reaches inside. "Why is she so pale?" asks Neve, taking Harlee. "And she's floppy."

"She was sick in the night. When I went in this morning, this is how she was."

"And you didn't call a doctor or think to bring her home?" snaps Neve, feeling Harlee's forehead. "She's burning up."

"She wouldn't quit whining so I left her to sleep it off," he tells her, pulling out Harlee's overnight bag. "Besides, you didn't answer my call so what was I supposed to do?"

"Leave a fucking message so I know to call back." She snatches the bag. "You can't have her overnight again, Finn. You don't know how to care for her properly."

I feel proud as she squares her shoulders and delivers the news. I'm already walking over when he grabs her upper arm, twisting it and causing Neve to cry out. Her eyes connect with mine and Finn looks over, to see what she's looking for. I give a smug smile and he instantly releases his grip on her. She stumbles back and I catch her, taking her arm in my hand and checking the red mark. "Go inside, Siren," I whisper, kissing her lightly on the head.

"This better be a fucking joke," yells Finn. Neve rushes inside, ignoring him and his face reddens in anger. "Neve!" he screams. "Get back here."

"Now there's the face of a man who knows he's lost," I say, grinning.

"This is a joke, right?" he demands, "You're not fucking sleeping with my wife."

"She's not your wife, Finn. She's my old lady."

"Bullshit. That's fucking bullshit."

I can't resist twisting the knife a little so I smirk right before I tell him, "She fucks me good, Finn. I had to make her mine."

He growls, rage filling him and he throws a weak punch, missing me. I laugh at his attempt, landing one right back in the centre of his face. His nose bursts open, spraying blood down his shirt. "I'll have you back inside for assault," he warns.

"Then I should make it worth it," I growl, rearing back again. This time, someone grabs my fist and I turn to find Griff. "He ain't worth it, brother. Who will keep Neve warm at night if you're inside?"

"Once I tell her the truth about what you did to that woman, she'll run a mile," Finn sneers.

I scoff, turning back to him. "She knows everything, Finn, you're too late. And when I get the evidence I need, she'll know that final last detail. And then you'll be going down for so long, Harlee will forget your face and she'll be calling me Daddy."

Chapter Twelve

Neve

I lay Harlee on the couch but she doesn't even stir which worries me more. I find the Calpol and suck the right amount into the oral syringe and gently lift her head slightly before slipping it into her mouth and squirting it a small amount at a time, giving her a chance to swallow in between each small dose. I kiss her on the head and lie her back down, opening the nearest window in the hope a breeze will cool her down. I notice Finn getting into his car, driving away at speed and Ryder is with Griff. It's good to see the pair talking, since Ryder returned, I've not really seen them together at all.

Ryder eventually comes inside. "Griff's gone to get her some treats," he says, "I asked him to add Calpol to the list."

I smile gratefully. "Thanks, you didn't need to."

He goes over to where Harlee is sleeping and feels her forehead. "She's cooling down," he tells me and I nod in agreement. He then places a gentle kiss on her forehead and it melts my heart. "She looks just like you," he murmurs, stroking her hair away from her sweaty forehead.

"What did Finn say?" I ask casually. I can't deny I'm worried about his next move. They'll be no stopping him now he knows about Ryder.

"I reminded him who he's messing with."

"He's going to try and take her from me," I add, my voice wavering with emotion.

"He can try, but he won't win. Don't worry about it, Siren, I've got this," he says, coming to me and kissing me on the forehead. "Go sit with your baby and I'll make you a drink."

I want to believe him, but I know Finn too well, he will stop at nothing to show me who's really in charge. Today was a small win but it won't last. He'll make sure of it.

Griff returns and he looks like his usually goofy self. He hands me the bag of things to cheer Harlee up, most of which I can't give her without signing her up to a lifelong illness such as heart disease but I'm grateful for the gesture. He follows me to the kitchen, leaving Ryder watching over Harlee.

"How're things with you?" I ask casually.

He lifts himself up onto the counter. "If you're asking are me and Ryder okay, then yeah, we're good."

"Did you talk?"

He shakes his head. "We're not like that, Siren. Talking gives me the ick."

I laugh. "And things are good with you and Corey?"

He grins, "The best."

"How does he cope with you?" I ask, because I've wanted to ask since I found out he was seeing someone. "You're so . . . hyper."

"Corey is the opposite, which brings me calm. He manages me quite well, usually by sucki-"

"Sorry I asked," I cut in, before he can finish the sentence. "I get the picture."

"What about you and my brother?"

I fold my arms over my chest and lean back against the counter beside him. "He's full on," I admit and Griff laughs. "I feel like we somehow married and I didn't know."

"He likes to go in like a bull, he was never very patient."

"But, I'm really enjoying having him around. It's been a long time since I had a man around."

"Just be careful," says Griff, jumping down from the counter. "I'd hate to have to kill you if you hurt him." He gives me a wink then leaves.

By bedtime, Harlee has improved. She's spent the day lying on the couch with Ryder one side, and me the other. It's been a nice, relaxing day, and if Finn wasn't lurking in the back of my mind, I could have almost pretended this was my happy ever after.

I take Harlee to bed and when I get downstairs, Ryder is waiting to pounce. He wraps me in his arms and kisses me until my toes curl. "I've been wanting to do that all day," he growls, burying his nose into my hair and inhaling. "We need an early night," he adds, backing me towards the stairs.

"You're staying over?" I ask, arching a brow.

He grins. "I'm staying wherever you are from this night onwards."

His words make me feel warm inside and by the time we make it to the bedroom, we're both half naked. Ryder pushes me to lay on the bed, parting my legs and burying his face between them. I arch off the bed as his tongue works it's magic and I'm almost about to lose it when my mobile vibrates across the table. Ryder pauses, glancing up at me. "Don't even think about answering," he warns me, and he rubs circles on my clit. But it's no good now, the moments gone. The phone rings off but I bat Ryder's hand away, much to his annoyance.

"He probably wants an update on Harlee," I reason.

"Bullshit and you know it. He doesn't give a crap about Harlee."

"He's still her dad," I whisper, unable to stop the anxiety that's currently taken over my body.

"We're not doing this," snaps Ryder, crawling up my body and taking each of my wrists, holding them above my head. "You don't answer to him anymore." He kisses me, and for a second, I get distracted, wrapping my leg around his waist and tugging him closer. I feel him at my entrance and groan as he sinks into me. My mobile begins its vibrating dance again, but Ryder keeps my hands pinned beside my head, slamming into me harder and faster.

He pulls from me and takes my hand to his erection, wrapping it around and keeping his over the top, rubbing fast until he comes over my stomach.

He drops down beside me again, his breathing is fast and heavy. "Answer the fucking phone," he grits out.

"It's fine, he'll get bored," I mutter.

"Answer the damn phone, Neve. He ain't ruining our night with constant phone calls. Answer it."

I go to grab my top, I'm currently down to my underwear, but he snatches it away. "Nuh huh, if he's gonna video call, he gets to see the shit he doesn't want to."

I roll my eyes, taking my phone just as it begins to ring for the fourth time. I answer, positioning it so he can't see below my neckline. "You think I'll let you get away with what happened today?" Finn spits angrily. I notice the cut on the bridge of his nose and a swelling on his cheek.

"Don't you want to know how your daughter is?" I ask. My heart beats wildly in my chest.

"There is no way I'm letting you keep her now, not after this," he yells.

"It's not up to you," I mutter.

"Oh baby, you know I have people that can take her from you before sunrise," he threatens.

"I went back to the school," I snap. "I told them the truth, they know you hit her, it's all on record."

"And?" he growls.

"And no judge is going to let you take her after that." He laughs and I feel my panic rising. Ryder gently squeezes my knee in a reassuring manner.

"I'm a fucking lawyer, Neve," he screams. "Do you think any judge will listen to you over me? You're nothing but a hotel receptionist. These judges know me, we play golf together. I'm taking Harlee, trust me on that. By the time I tell them about your murderer boyfriend and how my daughter is around criminal gangs, they'll be begging me to take her." A tear leaks down my cheek and I glance at Ryder. "Holy shit is he there, in my bed?" snaps Finn. I shake my head. "Show me," he demands.

I sit straighter, using a hand gesture to tell Ryder to move out of camera view. He scoffs, snatching the telephone from me. "Of course I'm here, Finn, she's my ol' lady, or wasn't that clear from our conversation today." I groan, burying my face in my hands. "If I remember right, Ryder, you owe me a woman already. I'm taking mine back and I'll return her broken and messed up along with that little brat. I have a special place just for them, mother and daughter, I might even mention that to the judge, you know how these guys work right? The right offer at the right time..." he trails off, leaving the sentence hanging in the air.

"That sounded like an admission, Finn. Why would I owe you a woman?"

Finn gives a small laugh. "I'm coming for her, Ryder. And then I'll take your club apart."

Ryder disconnects the call, throwing the handset on the bed and staring at it. After a few minutes, he looks at me. "Don't ever ask me to fucking hide from him again." He's angry, I can tell by the pulsing vein in the side of his neck and the way he clenches his jaw.

"I don't know what to do anymore," I cry.

He swoops down closer, pushing his face into mine and placing a hand either side of my thighs. "Stop falling at his feet," he growls, "Stop acting like he holds all the cards. You belong to me, Neve. You. Belong. To. Me."

His words should terrify me, but they send a thrill through me. I want to be owned by this man. I wrap my arms around his neck and kiss him hungrily. He makes no move to touch me back, so I push up onto my knees. "Show me," I whisper against his mouth.

"Show you?"

"That I belong to you."

He growls, sweeping me into his arms and wrapping my legs around his hips. "You drive me crazy," he whispers against my mouth.

I smile "You should punish me for that," I reply, arching a suggestive brow.

Ryder

Every time with Neve is different. We go from making love to fucking like starved animals. But that was by far the best fuck I've ever had in my life. We're lying side by side, staring up at the ceiling, with the sound of our heavy breaths filling the silence. "Do you trust me?" I ask.

I feel her turn her head to look at me. "Yes."

"I want you to move into the club."

She gives a laugh and when she sees I'm serious, she turns on to her side. "What?"

"I can keep you and Harlee safe there."

"We're safe here, aren't we?"

"At the club, you'll never be alone. There are always people around to keep you safe. I think we need to take extra steps since he's threatened you."

"He always threatens me," she says, frowning. "It's nothing new."

"But this time, you're not going to give in. He'll make more threats when he sees he's losing the grip he had on you. And he might carry them out if you're easy to get to."

She sits fully upright. "What do you mean? You said you were dealing with that."

"This is me dealing with it," he explains.

"Won't me taking Harlee into a biker club make him angrier?"

"I can keep you safer there, Neve. Just trust me."

By the following morning, I can tell Neve is more nervous. She spent the entire night tossing and turning and when it was finally time to get up, she rushed out before I had the chance to pin her down and fuck her slow.

I call the prospect to bring me a car and ask him to take my bike back. Then, while Neve packs a bag for her and Harlee, I call Griff.

"Jesus, Pres, it's nine in the morning," he grumbles sleepily.

"I thought I owed you a conversation," I tell him and I hear rustling his end, like he's getting out of bed. "I'm taking Neve and Harlee to the clubhouse."

"To show them around?" he asks.

"No, brother, I'm thinking of making this a permanent thing. I wanna claim her."

"Shit, Ryder. Where the fuck did this come from?"

"She's it, man. I ain't looking elsewhere."

"Well you know I like her, and the kids great, so I'm happy for you brother. Really happy. I'll come over and give you a hand."

Neve

We arrive at the clubhouse. It's pretty much how I imagined it to look on the outside. There are three large shutters, two at each end are pulled down but the middle one is lifted halfway, giving us access. Inside, there's a bar to the left. Ryder clears his throat to gain his attention but it doesn't work, he continues to stare up at the small television hung on the wall. "Whiskey, this is Neve," says Griff. He looks over, giving a slight nod of his head. He then picks Harlee up, "And Harlee," he adds. She nuzzles her head into his neck and closes her eyes like she's shy.

"She's under my protection Whisky, you spread that around for me," adds Ryder and the old guy gives a salute in acknowledgment.

Ryder turns to me with a smirk, "Whisky don't talk, he had his tongue cut out when he was a kid so don't expect much from him. He's a great guy and he'll look after you, so you need anything, you see him." I give a nod, glancing around the bar area where there are wooden tables with four stools tucked neatly under each one. Ryder notices, "Whisky has a serious case of OCD, if you see a stool outta place or missing, put that shit back. He's smashed up the joint before now just because some crazy bastard stole a stool."

"Got it," I say, looking past the tables to the couches spread out, all pointing towards a large screen television hung up high on the wall. Ryder leads me in that directions and towards a large man laying on one of the couches. As we approach, he sits up, showing off crazy red hair and a bushy ginger beard. "Pres," he greets.

"Bear, this is my woman, Neve," Ryder replies.

"Aww she's a wee pretty little thing," he says, with a hint of a Scottish accent, "Is she your little one?" he adds, looking from me to Harlee.

I smile, nodding. "She sure is, Harlee. She's five." Griff hands her to Ryder and I groan. She's nodded off and I know I'll pay for that when she wakes.

"Great name," he says with a wink.

Ryder continues to lead me past the couches and towards some snooker tables. There are two more bikers there, one I recognise as Knox from one of Griff's parties and Ryder introduces the other as Smokey. So far, everyone seems nice and friendly and I begin to relax.

There are three doors at the back of the room. One is Ryders office. Next to that is something Griff refers to as their 'church' which Ryder then explains is what they call their meetings in the biker world. The final door leads to the stairs. The clubhouse has three stories, but Ryder takes me straight to the first floor. The passageway has six doors and Ryder opens the second to last one.

"We'll get some things tomorrow to make it more like home for Harlee, this room's right next to ours and has a connecting door, see..." he demonstrates the door which leads between the two rooms. "We can leave the door open tonight in case she wakes and wonders where the hell she is," he adds with a laugh, laying Harlee on the white cotton sheets and pulling the blanket over her sleeping form.

He then props the door open and we go into his bedroom. I take in the dark woods and black sheets, frowning. "I know it's not great, I haven't had a chance to decorate since I came home," he says, shifting from one foot to the other like a nervous teenager.

I reach up and kiss him on the cheek. "It's perfect," I tell him. "We can work on the décor," I add, winking.

Chapter Thirteen

Ryder

I wake suddenly, sitting up and looking around. Neve is curled up beside me, still sleeping despite the wild storm outside. Lighting illuminates the room and the rumble of thunder tells me I won't get back to sleep any time soon. Neve's kicked the blankets off so I reach over her and pull them back into place, placing a gentle kiss on her head before getting out of bed. I grab my jeans and pull them on, then head down to my office. It's three in the morning, so I've slept for longer than I usually would. I need to work out my next move with Finn, there's no way I can let him keep his hold over her.

"The storm wake you up too?" I look up and find Griff standing in the doorway.

"Yeah, thought I'd go over the paperwork for the gym while it's quiet. You okay?" It seems like we've been avoiding each other since I saw him, we've just kind of slotted back into club life like it never happened.

He comes into the office and takes a seat opposite my desk. "You must have questions."

I place my pen on the desk and lean back in my chair. "I guess."

"I'm sorry I didn't tell you. I didn't want to add to your stress."

"Or you were scared of my reaction?"

He laughs giving a nod. "That too. You're my big brother, what you think matters and I couldn't stand the thought of you being disappointed in me like Dad always seemed to be."

"That bastard was disappointed in the whole damn world." I take two glasses from his desk drawer followed by a bottle of whiskey. "When did you know?"

"I've always known Ryder, right from being a kid and not understanding your fascination with girls. But I knew for sure around eleven when I fancied the gym teacher, Mr Hale." I screw up my face in disgust, thinking back to that teacher. Griff laughs, "I never said I had good taste."

"And it's always been men?"

"Not always. I've fancied women and slept with a few. But now I'm older and wiser," he gives a laugh, "I realise I'm into men."

"You just don't seem..." I trail off unable to find the right words. The last thing I want to do is upset him but I wasn't prepared for this conversation.

"Gay?" Griff asks, laughing again, "Not all Gay men walk around swaying their hips and talking in a high-pitched voice. I'm the same as I've always been Ethan, I'm still Eric and I always will be."

I nod. He's right, this hasn't changed him or how I feel about him. "And you have a boyfriend?" I ask, wincing because the words feel so foreign in my mouth.

"No, I have hook ups but nothing serious and no one permanent, although Corey hangs around a lot. Speaking of permanent, You and Neve?"

I allow him to change the subject, I'll only ask for what he's willing to tell me. "She's it man, it's happened fast but I can't not be around her. Besides, Finn knows now which means she's a target, so I had to move faster than planned. We need to come up with a way to get rid of that bastard and keep Neve and Harlee safe."

"It's done brother, we'll protect them both. Announce it to the club tomorrow, they need to know you've taken an old lady officially."

I like the sound of that and I smile wide. "Sounds like a plan."

Neve

I wake and stretch out, smiling as I realise I'm in Ryder's bed. I glance to the side and see the empty space. I sit up and pull the sheets around my naked body just as the conjoining door opens and Harlee sticks her head in. "Good morning Popple. Did you sleep well?" I ask, patting the empty space next to me. She rushes over and climbs in.

"Yes. Why are we here? Can I still go to school?"

I hadn't thought much past staying here, it was all so rushed. Ryder had already mentioned me not going into work today but I hadn't thought of school. I give a nod, deciding I should keep her routine as normal as possible. "Yes, baby girl, you're going to school after breakfast. We're staying with Ryder for a while if that's okay?"

She gives me a toothy grin. "Breakfast," she repeats, her eyes lighting up.

We dress and head downstairs to the kitchen. The large table in the centre of the room could easily seat sixteen people comfortably but currently there are just five guys sat around it eating breakfast and chatting amongst themselves.

I head for Ryder who's sitting at the head of the table. As we get closer, he glances up, smiling wide and reaching out for me to hand over Harlee. She goes to him and he sits her on his lap. "I was thinking that today we could choose the paint for your new room?" he suggests. Harlee nods eagerly and he passes her a pancake.

"After school of course," I cut in.

"School?" repeats Ryder, "She can't go to school today."

"I can't let him change our life Ryder. Harlee needs to be in school, we need to keep the same routine." Griff shoots me a worried look and Ryder stands, passing Harlee over to Griff.

"Office," he mutters, and I sigh. I always seem to say the wrong thing.

Once inside he turns to me, "Do you know how serious this is? Do you even realise half the stuff your ex is involved in?"

"Yes, I've lived with the threat of Finn for years. He won't hurt Harlee."

"He'll take her, Neve. He has too many big people on his side. You said yourself he would take her just to destroy you and now he knows about us we've given him the perfect opportunity."

"What do you want us to do? Hide away here forever?" I ask, giving an unamused laugh.

"Finnegan Lawrence is a monster. Not the kind that you can afford to ignore hoping he'll get bored. I can drive you around the streets today and take you to girls that will run and hide if you mention his name to them. I can point out all the whore houses that he run's illegally and not one girl will speak out against him in fear that he'll kill them."

I frown, feeling confused. I know he's no angel, but seriously, people fear him? I can't imagine him murdering anyone. "All that might be true, but he still wouldn't hurt Harlee."

"Neve he doesn't give a shit about Harlee, if someone offered a good price for her, he'd sell her, and you'd never see her again."

I scoff. "Don't be ridiculous, that's his daughter and I know he's a lot of things, but he wouldn't hurt his own flesh and blood."

"He's a rapist," he hisses, angrily. I swallow the lump in my throat. "He instils fear into weak women and then controls them to do what he wants. He makes money from foreign girls that he's arranged to bring over to this country by selling them to pimps and forcing them into his whore houses. I can almost guarantee that he rubbed his dirty hands together when you gave birth to a girl!"

"Stop, he wouldn't do anything bad to Harlee," I snap.

"Please just listen to me Neve, I ain't making this shit up. I'll make sure that Harlee doesn't miss out on her schooling but until I can figure out what to do, I need you to listen and stay here. Neither of you are safe outside of this clubhouse."

My phone buzzes in my back pocket, making me jump. I pull it out and roll my eyes, pointing it towards Ryder so he can see Finn's name. "Answer it," he orders.

I sigh, pressing it to my ear. "Finn?"

"Have you seen sense yet?" His voice is cold and distant.

"Why are you calling me?"

"Do you know how mad I was finding out you're fucking a dirty gang leader. It makes me sick to know you're letting him touch you. He's a dog yah know, he'll use you and break your heart."

"If you haven't called for any specific reason, I'm hanging up."

"Don't you dare fucking hang up on me. Did he tell you that just the other night he was having sex with one of my girls. He paid for a private dance, there's no limits in those private rooms and he likes a bit of kinky fuckery." I remain quiet, I trust Ryder. And Finn will say anything to make me leave here, but still, there's a niggling doubt at the back of my mind. "He'll lie of course, but you always do fall for the liars and cheats. Jesus, you believed everything I told you. I wanted to slap you for being so stupid."

"You did slap me, several times. I have to go."

"You're running late for school get a move on."

"Unless you need to speak to me about Harlee, then please don't call me."

"Is that your boyfriend's rules? You let him know that I make the damn rules, especially when it comes to you and my daughter. I'll see you in court. Pack Harlee's clothes, I'm taking her."

Ryder takes the mobile from me and cancels the call. "What did he say?" he asks.

"Nothing important. The usual bullshit."

It's been a weird kind of day. I've spent time getting to know some of the women. Mainly Kit and Sia, who belong to Knox and Smokey. Sia and Smokey also have a daughter aged six, which meant we had enough in common to chat the morning away.

And for the last hour, I've been sat at the bar playing cards with Whiskey. "Didn't anyone ever teach you to sign, Whiskey?" I ask, and he shakes his head.

Sia told me he lost his tongue when he was just a kid, which made no sense to me. He's spent his entire life struggling to communicate when he could have been taught sign language to at least offer him some kind of strategy. "I know some, can I teach you?" He eyes me for a moment with suspicion, then he shrugs and gives a nod. I grin, placing my cards on the table. "Great." And I set about teaching him some basics.

An hour passes when I notice Ryder pass us to step outside. He returns minutes later with Miss Hind following him. It shouldn't bother me, seeing them together. But since Finn said those words, I've been feeling less confident and she is really pretty. "Siren, I got Harlee some extra tuition." He smiles wide, like he's holding the key to all the answers, but I don't feel the same and his smile falters when he realises it.

"Oh my god, tell me that's not Sass," came a loud voice. Bear rushes her from behind and picks her up, spinning her around. It's the first time I've seen her smile and it only makes her look more beautiful. I roll my eyes.

"Hey Bear, long time no see. How's the kids?"

"Ochs, there's too many of them now, we're on baby number seven."

"That poor wife of yours." She laughs, shaking her head.

"Let me take you to the kitchen. The guys'll be pleased to see you." She goes off with Bear and Ryder follows, probably realising I'm pissed.

I watch Sarah working with Harlee from my seat at the bar. It seems that Harlee loves the one-on-one approach and is concentrating so hard as she chews on her pencil. It's hard not to notice how Ryder is also hanging around her, occasionally speaking in her ear whenever Harlee is writing something down. The sense in me knows it's nothing. He wouldn't be sat with my daughter, chatting his ex up. But the jealous part of my brain hates it.

"You look like a sad puppy dog waiting to be rehomed." Griff sits down beside me munching happily on an apple.

"I do not," I snap, sulkily.

"You do so. She's the mother of his child, he just wants to win her over so he can see Alfie."

"How far would he go to do that?"

"How far would you go to see Harlee if she was taken from you? He wants Sass to see that he's changed, he's grown up and he's sticking around."

His words are not helping and I arch a brow. "And he thought he'd use my daughter to do that?"

"No, he promised you he'd get Harlee sorted so that she didn't miss out on school."

Harlee runs towards us waving a piece of paper. "Look what I did," she bellows excitedly.

Griff picks her up and takes the paper from her so that we could look at it together. I look up as Ryder heads for his office, with Sarah hot on his heels.

Griff catches me watching and smiles, "It's not what you think. He likes you."

Ryder

It's early evening when I finally sit down on the worn couch. I turn my eyes to where Neve is teaching Whiskey to sign. It's one of my new favourite things to watch and as she throws her head back laughing, before repositioning Whiskey's fingers, I find myself smiling.

I know she's being off with me. She's hardly spoken since I walked in with Sassy. But I ain't gonna apologise for keeping Harlee learning. This morning Neve was complaining her daughter would miss school, and now she was mad I'd found a solution. Besides, it wasn't my idea. I'd called Sassy first thing to explain the situation and she'd offered. The Griff had pointed out it was a good way to get into Sassy's good books, so I took the chance, hoping it'll lead to me being able to see Alfie.

"Neve," I call, and she glances over her shoulder at me. "Come," I add. She turns back to Whiskey, ignoring my command. I smile, there's something about her defiance that turns me on. "Siren, don't ignore me."

"I'm busy," she mutters, keeping her back to me. Whiskey raises his eyebrows in surprise. It isn't often someone shows disrespect to his president.

"Two seconds to make it right or I'm doing it my way," I warn.

I watch as some of the guys trudge in, followed by the club girl's they've been to collect from the bar. They hang around the bikers and offer a good time for free rent and food. It's a win-win situation. Viv spots me and makes a beeline. I smirk, wondering if this will get Neve listening to me. I let her slide into the space beside me and place her hand over my knee, raking her red nails there. "How's my favourite president?" she purrs.

I grin, leaning my head back on the couch and closing my eyes. "All the better for seeing you, V."

I don't feel her presence until it's too late. A cold drink hits my face and Viv screams, jumping away from me. I sit up and stare into Neve's furious eyes. She's holding a now empty glass. "Do not play games with me, Ryder," she warns, angrily before stomping away.

I stare wide eyed, hardly believing she lost it like that. Griff laughs hard, clapping his hands together. "Man, she had more fire than I thought."

Whiskey throws me a towel and I wipe my face. "Shut the fuck up, Griff," I mutter. I get up and rush after her.

She's almost at our room by the time I catch her, wrapping an arm around her waist and pulling her against me. "You gonna pay for that, Siren," I whisper hiss. I wrestle her into our room and the second I close the door, she spins on her heel to face me, glaring in anger.

I take in her stance and keep my distance, "You look ready to fight, Siren." I sigh, adding in a gentler tone, "I'm not him, I won't hurt you."

She inhales sharply, and the anger leaves her expression. I step closer, pushing her against the wall and kissing her until I feel the last of it melt away. She begins to tug at my clothing and I shrug from my kutte. "I want to hear you screaming my name," I whisper, unfastening her button and pushing her jeans down her legs. She steps out of them. I grip her lace underwear and tear them from her, dropping them to the floor. "But first of all, I want to make it clear," he whisper, rubbing my fingers over her wet entrance. She closes her eyes, gasping in pleasure, "that I might talk to other women, some might be ex's or people I've had sex with, it doesn't mean I'm fucking them."

I unfasten my own jeans and free my cock, fisting my erection and crouching enough to line myself up at her entrance. "Hold on to me," I instruct, as I lift her slightly. "I'm yours. No matter what people say, what you think you see, I am yours." I thrust into her and she cries out in surprise.

"Seeing her here today threw me," she admits, gripping my shoulders as I slowly drag my cock from her, before easing back in. "She belongs here, I don't." Her cheeks colour slightly at her confession, like it slipped out without her permission.

I groan, "Siren, you belong here. Wherever I am, that's where you should be. Sassy is my past but you are my future." I move faster, enjoying the feel of her pussy choking me. "I want to see Alfie, to do that I have to break down her walls, but that doesn't mean I'm cheating on you."

"What if that's what she wants? What if she wants you to be a family?" I press my head against her shoulder trying to regain composure. This is the most she's opened up to me so far and I don't want to rush it.

"Then I'll tell her that I already have a family which I want Alfie to be a part of. Unfortunately, there's no room for Sassy in that."

Relief floods her face and she wraps her arms around my neck, shuddering as she comes apart. "You need to know that I like you a lot, I haven't felt like this in a long time and I plan to tell the club that you're mine. In my world that's huge, just as good as putting a ring on your finger."

Neve places her hands on my cheeks, staring intently into my eyes. "Thank you," she whispers, before kissing me slow and dragging an orgasm from me. I growl, stilling as I release into her. "I'm sorry I've been such a cow all day," she adds, placing kisses over my face. "Forgive me?"

"Always," I tell her, lowering her to the floor. I hand her a pair of boxers shorts, wondering if she'll comment on the fact we didn't use protection. It's not something we've discussed but I don't hate the idea of her carrying my kid. Fuck, when I picture it, it gets me hard. She slips the shorts on and slides into bed, pulling the sheets back for me to join her. I smile and snuggle up behind her.

Chapter Fourteen

Neve

It had been a week since I'd arrived at the club and I was finally starting to relax. Finn hadn't bothered to call me again, which was helping me to feel less anxious. Although deep down, I wasn't sure if it was a blessing or a curse, at least when he called, I knew what he was up to. However, Ryder had a new plan, and we'd decided that doing it all illegally wasn't going to work, we need to prove without a doubt that Harlee is safer with me. Our main problem was that I've never reported Finn for any of the abuse and the only record of anything happening was the school's safeguarding concern. It's frustrating that it isn't enough, surely one time hitting a child is plenty, but Ryder thinks we need more.

I take a breath and head over to where Sarah is working with Harlee. I have to make the effort with her if I want her to accept I'm a part of Ryder's life, because hopefully, I'll also be a part of Alfie's. "Do you want a drink?" I ask.

"No, where's Ryder"? she asks, her tone unfriendly.

"He's just at the gym. Can I help?"

"He's supposed to be coming over tonight for dinner. We need to discuss Alfie."

I stiffen at her words, he hadn't mentioned dinner. "Well, I'm sure he hasn't forgotten."

Sarah smiles, arching a brow. She crosses her legs and her short skirt rides up enough to show she's wearing stockings held by suspenders. *Who would wear that to school?* "He'd better not have, I've brought his favourite dinner in."

I force a smile before walking away. I won't bite and it's clearly what she wants. As I take a seat at the bar, Ryder comes in looking flushed from his workout. He spots me and heads over, kissing me on the head. "Good day?" he asks. I nod. "I've had the afternoon from hell."

"Sassy is waiting for you," I mutter, trying to sound less bothered than I am.

He groans, "Oh crap, I forgot to tell you, I'm going over to hers to talk about Alfie."

I nod, keeping my eyes fixed on the television. "Yeah, I heard."

"Sorry, It slipped my mind," he says, kissing me on the head for a second time. I don't respond and he sighs heavily before trudging off in Sarah's direction.

I watch as he greets her warmly, and then Harlee reaches up and he pulls her into his arms while chatting with Sarah.

"You ready?" he asks.

Sarah nods, gathering up her things. "Is steak still your favourite?"

He looks delighted. "Man, you know it, but seriously you don't have to cook."

She rolls her eyes, "You've been at work. A home cooked meal is just what you need."

Her words niggle at me. I haven't cooked one meal for Ryder, he often orders in or snacks, but I've never seen him eat a good meal. He heads back to me, handing Harlee over. "I'll be back in an hour or so," he tells me. I nod and he rolls his eyes in irritation before following Sarah out.

An hour turns to two, then three, then four and by eleven, I'm annoyed. I shouldn't be. I have no right to be. Ryder's done nothing to make me doubt him and he's reassured me so much, more than any other man would bother to do. I eventually drift off to sleep, where I mainly dream of Ryder being swayed by Sarah's stocking clad legs. I wake with a start when I hear him stumble into the bedroom. He curses before chuckling to himself. I glance at the bedside clock to see it's almost one in the morning. "Ryder?" I whisper, turning on the lamp. He's holding on to the wall for support and he gives me a stupid grin. "I was worried."

He pushes off the wall and falls face first onto the end of the bed. "Yeah, it took longer than I thought."

"Did you manage to sort anything out about Alfie?" He chuckles again and shrugs his shoulders. "Wasn't that the point?"

"Yeah, but then Sass opened a bottle of my favourite whiskey and we got reminiscing. You know, there was a time when she was my bestest friend," he mutters, almost wistfully.

"Great," I huff, lying back down and kicking my feet into his ribs. He grunts but doesn't move.

"Are you mad with me?" He sounds amused.

"Should I be?"

"I was catching up with an old friend," he says, turning onto his side and dragging himself to his half of the bed. "I told you a million times, there's nothing to worry about."

"Right, but then you go for a chat about your son and end up coming home hours later, shit faced. Good night, Ryder."

He sighs heavily and I pull the sheets up to my chin. I can't help how I feel.

I kiss Harlee on the head and she rushes off in the direction of her friends. "Have a great day, Popple."

This morning I'd woken with a fresh mind and the intention of getting my life back on track. I need routine and so does Harlee. Ryder had groaned and covered his head with the pillow when I'd tried to wake him to discuss it, so I'd gone ahead and made my own decision, after all, I'm a grown woman and I can do as I please.

I'd quit the job at the hotel but I knew exactly where I'd be welcomed, and as I push open the door to the florist, Mollie smiles wide. "Hey Neve." She dropped her cutting tool and the rose stem and rounded the counter to hug me in greeting. "How are you?"

"I'm good. I needed to get out the house. Do you need a hand?"

"Oh my god, if you're serious, I could kiss you right now. I have a tonne of orders." She nodded towards the pile of note paper on the worktop.

"I'll get stuck in then." I take my things into the back room and swap my jacket for an apron.

"Weren't there any extra shifts at work?" Mollie asks when I rejoin her.

"I quit. It's a long story involving bikers, Finn, and a not very understanding boss."

"Oh, that's not good. How will you manage financially?"

"Ryder's helping me out," I tell her wincing. "I'll get back on my feet when things have died down with Finn."

"Okay, fill me in," she says, and I do. I tell her everything that led me to this point and she stares open mouthed.

"Christ Neve, your life is like a soap drama. Are you sure Harlee is safe at school?"

"Yes. I'm going early to collect her, and all of the teachers know that she is not to be released to her Dad."

My phone rings out and I see Ryders name and groan. I'm surprised it took him two hours to be honest, so I paste a smile on my face and answer, making sure to sound relaxed and breezy.

"Hi Ryder."

"Don't you dare tell me you're out without an escort?"

"I am out without an escort. Harlee is at school and..."

"What?" he roars.

"She needs routine and-"

"She needs to be safe and that's why we agreed you'd both stay here."

"Why are you yelling?"

"Because you drive me nuts, Neve. I'm doing everything I can to keep you both safe and you ignore me. Is this because of last night?"

"No."

"I feel like it is. If Harlee is in school, you won't need to have Sassy around?"

"Don't be ridiculous," I mutter, my cheeks reddening at my obvious jealousy. "She's my daughter and I make those decisions."

The line goes silent and I glance at the screen to make sure we're still connected. He clears his throat and then says, "Message received loud and clear, Neve. Apologies for overstepping."

I sigh, hating that he's hurt by my words. "Look sorry, I just meant..."

"I know exactly what you meant, Neve. Forget it. I'm seeing Alfie tonight so I don't know if I'll be here when you get home."

"For an hour or six?" I ask, unable to hold back.

He scoffs. "Right. I should go before we both end up saying something we'll regret."

I'm not ready for him to go and so I blurt words out before fully thinking them through. "Actually, I was thinking I should probably go home, as in back to my own place." I regret them instantly and wince, waiting for his reply.

"Right. Whatever you want, Neve."

He disconnects and I stare at the blank screen. My heart twists painfully and I bite my inner cheek to stop myself from crying. It doesn't work and tears form in my eyes.

"That sounded like a breakup," says Mollie gently. "Are you okay?"

I shrug, it felt like one, that's for sure. "He's trying to get to know his son and deep down I know he likes me, but I feel threatened by his ex. She's beautiful and they have history."

"Why are you talking like you're not beautiful?" she demands, rubbing my arm. "You're gorgeous, Neve. Don't let your insecurities ruin this."

"But they didn't fall out of love and break-up, he cheated on her. There's so much unfinished business between them but it never got sorted because he went to prison. Now he's back..." I trail off, realising that I'm rambling. "And I don't feel beautiful at side of her. She hated me when she was just Harlee's teacher, but now she knows about me and Ryder, she looks like she wants to kill me."

"Has Ryder given you any reason to doubt him?" I shake my head sadly. "Then stop letting trust issues ruin what you have. It sounds to me like the guy's doing everything he can to make you happy, Neve, which is more than Finn ever did."

I groan, burying my face in my hands. "I think I've just blown it now, he's sick of me and I don't blame him."

"You've spent too long playing games because you had to survive Finn. Ryder isn't the same. You can relax and enjoy this relationship. Not everything will end in arguments and violence."

Ryder
I've spent the entire day yelling at people. The second I woke up and realised Neve had been gone for most of the morning, I just knew it would end badly, and that wasn't helped by the massive hangover. I tracked Neve's mobile to a florist and sent a prospect to watch her. Forcing her back here when we're both pissed, won't make things better, so I'll give her time to cool off, but that doesn't mean I won't watch her every move. The other prospect is stationed outside Harlee's school, watching for any signs of that prick turning up.

And now, I was sat outside Sassy's nice house, feeling nervous. I don't think I've ever felt fucking nervous in my life, but meeting Alfie feels huge.

The front door opens and Sassy stands there smiling at me. Her long white flowing dress almost makes her look like a saint. She's a vision of beauty, she always had been. I make my way to her and hold out the small bunch of flower's I'd picked up from the shop up the road. It wasn't planned but I felt bad coming empty handed. I also got it on good authority from Harlee, that five-year-old boys like Paw Patrol, and so the gift for Alfie is tucked safely under my arm.

Sassy opens the door wider for me to go inside, "I wondered how long you were going to sit out here for," she teases.

"I was just gathering myself," I mutter, and she points for me to go through to the living room.

I swallow the huge lump in my throat when my eyes land upon the small dark haired little boy, and relief floods me when I see he's watching a huge dog on television, just like the one I've brought him. "It's his favourite show, he won't respond to either of us until its finished," says Sassy with a smile, "Coffee?" I nod, following her into the kitchen. "How was your head this morning? We finished the whole bottle off," she says, grabbing two cups. "Reminded me of old times."

"It was sore," I admit. "I couldn't get my backside out of bed." My mind wonders to Neve. She was right to be pissed last night. I didn't even call to tell her I would be so late. I was too wrapped up in impressing Sass so she'd let me see my kid. I pull out my mobile and check for messages, when I see nothing, I dial the prospect. "Just gotta make a quick call," I tell Sassy as she stirs the coffee.

He answers straight away, "They're both home Pres, she picked the kid up early from school and she's been in the house since."

"Thanks, I'll be there later. Stay posted until I arrive." I disconnect and Sassy hands me a coffee.

"Everything okay?"

"All's good."

"You seem distracted," she pushes. "Is it anything to do with Harlee and her Mum? I noticed she was back in school today."

"I'm not distracted, I'm fine," I snap. I take a calming breath. "I just want to meet my kid."

"We can do it another time if you've got places to be," she says, arching a brow.

I exhale, "It's been a long day, not helped by the hangover. I'm not in a rush, I'm just tired."

Before she can reply, Alfie runs through and Sassy gathers him in her arms, placing kisses over his face. "So, remember I told you that a special person was coming to meet you tonight?" she asks. Alfie nods, staring at me with curiosity. "Well this is Mummy's friend, Ryder."

"You have a funny name," says Alfie, his voice barely a whisper.

I smile. "My real name is Ethan. Ryder is my biker name." I slide the present across the worktop towards him, "I got you a present."

Sassy places him on the worktop and he opens the paper wrapping, gasping at the cuddly dog. "Wow, that's the one you wanted," says Sassy, looking impressed. "Good gift."

"Thank you," says Alfie, grinning whilst cuddling the toy.

Neve

I tuck Harlee's blankets around her soft, warm body, adding a gentle goodnight kiss to her forehead before turning out the lamp. She's spent the last half hour crying for Ryder, and I'd almost caved and called him for her, but then realised I couldn't spend the next few weeks doing that, I'd never get over him. I guess we both need to get used to not having him around.

I get downstairs and do a quick tidy up of Harlee's toys before sitting at the kitchen table and opening my laptop. If I'm going to be an independent woman again, I need a job. Part of me wants to leave London and start again, but the thought of that is scary, especially alone.

Emails ping, getting my attention and I open the link, realising they're from a dating app I'd signed up to one drunken night after my split from Finn. I smile at the email telling me I have new activity on my account and my curiosity peaks. It can't hurt to look. I make myself a coffee then begin sifting through the men I've been matched with.

"You moving on already?" Ryder's deep voice rumbles through me and I scream in fright, jumping up off my chair to find him standing at the back door.

"Christ Ryder, you scared the shit out of me."

He saunters over, peering at the laptop. "Like's walks in the park and romantic nights in," he reads aloud. "Looking for younger woman to put the spark back into life." Ryder rolls his eyes, "Desperate."

"How did you get in?" I demand, even though I'm secretly thrilled to see him.

"Why are you on dating sites?"

"It came up on my email, it's an old profile, I was just being nosey."

"Or looking to replace me?" He arches an accusing brow as I lower back into my seat and click off the site.

"Did you see Alfie?"

"He's the double of me when I was that age," he says with a smile. "He's a cute little kid."

"You'll get to see him more then?" What I'm asking is if he'll see more of Sarah, which is stupid because of course he will.

"Siren I've told you over and over, you have nothing to worry about. Let's talk about today and you going AWOL."

"Let's talk about you going out last night and going AWOL until the early hours, at which point you returned drunk." He smirks and I know he's turned on by my anger. I sigh, "I need my job, I need my independence and I have a responsibility to Harlee."

"Yes, you do, to keep her safe. What you did today put her at risk."

"I can't live my life hiding from Finn. He hasn't hurt her before I don't see why he would now," I reason.

"Because now you're with me and he hates me."

I groan aloud, we're going around in circles. "I need my own money."

"I'll give you money," he offers.

"I want my own money, from a job. I need to take care of Harlee myself. It's not that I don't appreciate you helping me, but Finn did that once and then he left, and I didn't have a clue how to pay bills. I've spent a long time making myself independent."

His expression softens. "Fine, I'll give you a job at the club, cleaning, cooking, whatever you want to do."

"No, that's not what I meant."

He growls in frustration. "Look, you want a job and I need help around the club. Take the job so we can move forward. I can keep you safe at the club, I can't keep you safe if you stay here."

I close the laptop. "I thought we were over, you were so mad earlier."

Ryder takes my chin in his fingers, forcing me to look at him. "I told you that I'm not going anywhere. Whatever happens I'm here to stay. What do I need to do to prove that?" I shrug helplessly. Ryder could have his pick of women, the club girls are always around him hoping to get noticed. Why the hell would he want me when I come with all this baggage. He kisses me on the lips. "I don't know what else to do, baby. I'm yours, you're mine, that's it. No one else can come close. I'm only interested in you."

"Why?" I ask.

He frowns, "Why do I want you?" I nod. He smiles, "you're amazing, Neve. Everything about you is from the tip of your nose," he kisses me there, "To the tips of your toes. I don't see past you, Neve. You're it for me."

"What happened last night?" I ask, breaking the eye contact.

He sighs, "I spent time catching up with Sassy. Before all the shit, we were good together, friends. We lost that after what I did. So we talked over a bottle of whiskey, and I should have considered how that'd make you feel, I'm sorry for that. But I'm new to this too, I'm still learning. And I'll fuck up a lot, just like you will, but it doesn't mean that every time we argue, we're splitting up. I want your profile off that dating site now and tomorrow, we'll make us official the way of the club."

"Official?" I repeat. It's not the first time he'd mentioned it but I didn't have a clue what he meant.

He grins. "It means parties, tattoos and a whole lot of biker love. I should have made it a priority but shits been crazy. After we're official, you'll see how serious I am about us."

Chapter Fifteen

Ryder

Neve reaches for the pillow and buries her face into it, groaning as I ram into her at a punishing rate. We've spent most of the night like this, wrapped up in one another, and still it's not enough. Arguing with her puts me on edge, I hate the thought of her being upset because of me so maybe this urge is to prove to us both, that we're good together.

I come, growling as the tension leaves me. If I haven't put a baby in her belly by the end of the week, I'll be shocked. I fall beside her and she rolls into my side placing her hand on my clammy chest. "You didn't use protection again," she whispers sleepily.

"Your point?" I ask, grinning.

"I'll get the morning after pill and enquire about getting the pill or something."

I take her hand in mine, entwining our fingers. "That won't be needed."

"Don't you think it's a little soon to be having a baby?" she asks, laughing.

"Nope, I keep telling you that I'm yours and you're mine, what part of that don't you get?"

"We had our first major argument today, Ryder. We practically spilt up."

"We definitely didn't split up, I just let you cool down for a few hours."

"Still, it's a huge commitment."

"Don't you want more kids?" I ask.

She thinks over my words. "Yeah, I've always wanted more. And I guess Harlee is at a nice age now, but we haven't been together long enough. I don't fancy being a single mum to two kids."

"You'll never be single again. Look, If it happens, then it happens. It's Gods wish."

She laughs, tapping my chest playfully. "No, it's us not taking precautions. We're being irresponsible, that's nothing to do with God."

"It's how they did things in the olden days," I say, shrugging. "Stop overthinking it."

"Yeah when women stayed home with ten kids and the men worked in the coal pits. Times have changed."

I roll onto my side and tuck her hair away from her face. "The thought of you pregnant with my kid makes me happy, and ten kids would be amazing."

She laughs again, "Not a chance, Ryder. I will not have ten little Ryders running around in this world, think of the poor women. It's our duty to the world not to produce too many Ryders."

I grin, slapping her backside. "So cheeky."

Somewhere in my dream like state I hear glass breaking. I feel Neve nudging me and then she hisses my name in a desperate whisper. I open one eye. "Huh?"

"I heard a noise," she whispers.

I roll onto my back and check the time. It's four in the morning. I can't hear anything but I throw my legs over the bed and slip my jeans on. I reach into my boot and pull out my knife.

"Stay here," I whisper.

I step out into the hall and listen again. The lights are out and there's no sign of torches or any sounds coming from anywhere. I move carefully, making sure to stay back against the wall. I low thud has me freezing and suddenly, a ginger cat runs past me, confusing me for a second. Neve's never mentioned a cat before. "Ryder, you came?" Harlee stands in her doorway rubbing her eyes sleepily.

I glance back at the stairs where the cat ran, before tucking my knife in my back pocket before scooping Harlee into my arms and going back into her room. "What are you doing up baby girl"? I whisper. "Let's get you back to bed." I make a mental note to ask Neve about the cat.

"Will you be here when I wake up?" she asks as I tuck her in.

"Of course," I promise.

Harlee's expression changes from happy to horrified, in a split second. Then a sharp pain radiates through my skull and the last thing I hear is Harlee screaming and my eyes close.

Neve

I dive up from the bed the second I hear Harlee scream. I'd dressed while Ryder had gone off to check and as I rush towards her room, with my heart thudding in my chest, I call out for Ryder.

I freeze at the sight of Finn holding our daughter who is sobbing uncontrollably, desperately trying to get free. My eyes fall to Ryder and I gasp out loud as I take in his lifeless body.

He's bleeding from his head and the crimson fluid surrounds him, soaking into the pink fluffy carpet.

"I told you I was coming, Princess," Finn sneers.

"Give Harlee to me." I hold out my shaking arms, desperately reaching for her but he pulls her tighter into his chest.

"I'm going to tell you exactly what's going to happen next, Neve. If you give me any trouble, I'll take off her fingers one by one, is that clear?" I nod, not daring to argue. A large man appears behind me and I shrink away as Finn passes Harlee to him. She screams and I force a reassuring smile.

"It's okay baby, everything is going to be okay just calm down."

"There's a car waiting for us downstairs. You do anything stupid and I won't hesitate to carry out my threat," says Finn.

"Please, Finn, let me take Harlee. She's upset and if you take her out in this state, the neighbours will hear. Let me carry her and I can keep her calm."

Finn nods his head once and the large man hands Harlee to me. I sigh in relief, squeezing her tight, and pushing her face into the crook of my neck so she doesn't have to look at Ryder anymore. "Shhh," I soothe. "You're okay, mummy's got you."

The large man leads the way and I follow with Finn trailing behind. I pray that for once, Griff is home. I mean, it's unlikely seeing as he's been talking of selling the place. Since he came out to the club, he doesn't need to hide away anymore.

I stare at his house as I slide into the waiting car, but his lights are all out, dashing my hopes. I place Harlee into the child seat and secure her, taking a hold of her hand and gently rubbing it. Finn slides in beside me, gripping my knee. "Good girl," he praises.

We drive for at least half an hour before stopping at the metal gates of a large stately looking house. A man dressed in a suit approaches, opening the gates and we go through.

I get Harlee from her seat, she's fast asleep, probably worn out from all the crying. I follow Finn out of the car and up the stone steps leading to the large door, which opens as we approach. Another man in a suit stands patiently whilst we file in. Finn turns to him, "Dennis, is Mary still around?" The man nods whilst taking Finn's jacket. "Great, have her stay so she can meet my family."

"Very well, Mr Lawrence."

"I'm just going to show them to their room."

He takes the winding staircase, knowing I'll follow. I stare after him in disbelief, he's acting like all this is normal, like he didn't just beat my boyfriend over the head. Tears threaten to fall again when I picture Ryder lying there lifeless.

We stop outside one of the rooms and Finn opens it with a key. He stands to one side, indicating for me to go in first which I do. I stare at the king-sized bed, the white cotton sheets look crisp and fresh and I fight the urge to slide under them and close my eyes in the hope this is all a bad dream. I turn towards the French doors and hope ignites inside, maybe once he's gone, I could climb out of those? He sees me staring and laughs before marching over to them and pushing on them. They don't budge. "They're locked, Neve, do you think I'm stupid?"

"What are you trying to achieve, Finn? I don't understand," I ask as I lay Harlee onto the bed and pull a blanket over her. She doesn't even stir and I pray that by the time she wakes, I've figured a way to get us out of here.

"I just want my family back together," he says with a smug grin.

"Why? You haven't wanted us for years. In fact, I don't think you want us at all, you just don't want anyone else to have us."

"If you hadn't have broken the rules, we wouldn't be in this situation."

"Rules?" I scoff, glancing at Harlee to make sure I haven't woken her. I step closer to him, glaring angrily, "You don't get to lay down the rules when you've left, Finn. That's not how the break-up works."

His smile fades and a darkness takes over his eyes as he grips me around the throat. I close my eyes and concentrate on breathing through my nose. I've learnt over the years that if I don't panic, I can get through this. "The rules were there for a reason, Neve. You belong to me." He shoves me back a step, releasing me. "Now," he says, more calmly this time whilst he straightens his shirt. "Let's meet my staff."

Staff. He has staff? When we were together, we spent all our time in the luxury apartment he owned in London. Now suddenly he has this huge house and *fucking* staff? I give Harlee one last glance before begrudgingly following him back downstairs.

We go into the kitchen and I almost gasp out loud at the size of it. The units are all white with a marble worktop. The fridge is enormous and right now, none of it's making any sense to me. An older looking lady is sitting at the table sipping a cup of something hot. "Mary, this is my wife, Neve." She smiles tightly, giving a slight nod in greeting.

"Separated," I add, arching a defiant brow.

Finn ignores me and continues, "Mary will bring your meals to your room. The only time you can leave the room is if I am with you."

I roll my eyes, "Are you kidding me? You want to keep me locked away with a five-year-old?"

"Think yourself lucky I've put you in a nice bedroom, and not downstairs," he retorts, pointing to a white door across the room.

I stare at the giant padlock on it. "What's downstairs?"

"Keep asking annoying questions and you'll find out."

Finn makes quick work of showing me the rest of downstairs. The grand living room, the dining room with a table that seats twenty guests. I want to point out that he doesn't have twenty people that would want to willingly sit down to dinner with him, but I stay quiet. By the time he walks me back to the bedroom, I'm relieved to be getting away from him. The house tour was nothing more than a chance to show off, because clearly I won't get to spend time anywhere but in this room.

I wait for him to leave, locking the door, and then I climb into bed beside Harlee and allow myself to break down.

Ryder

I groan and roll onto my side. A searing pain rips through my head and I grip it, feeling my hair is matted. I glance around and see the dried blood around me, immediately sitting up and regretting the sudden move. The room spins and I groan, feeling my head again and running my fingers over the oozing cut. And then my memories hit me like a sledgehammer. Harlee screaming. The cat. And him, fucking Finn. "Neve," I call out, gripping on to Harlee's empty bed and pulling myself on to my knees. I know they're both gone. Of course they are. But I still shout her name again and again as I stand and hold onto the wall for support. I carefully make my way back to Neve's bedroom. It's empty, just like I expected.

I grab my mobile from the bedside cabinet and open the tracking app. It shows Neve's phone as being here, at the house. I growl in frustration. I dial Griff's number.

"Brother, where are you, yah dirty stop out," he answers.

"Griff, I need you," I mumble, sitting on the edge of the bed and gripping my head again. The pain is unbelievable and my vision blurs. "Neve has . . ." I can't think straight and I lie back, closing my eyes. "Brother, I-" And then everything goes black.

The sunrise blazed through the French doors. Not that it mattered, I'd laid here wide awake since Finn left me here. The constant worry over Ryder keeping me tossing and turning. What if he was dead? What if no one found him for days? Would Griff worry if he hadn't heard from either of us? Probably not right away because he'd be giving us time to sort our shit out.

Harlee's eyes suddenly shot open and she instantly began to cry. I snuggle against her, whispering comforting words.

"I want to go home," she says between sniffles.

"Me too baby," I whisper.

"Will Daddy hurt us?" The words cause a lump in my throat, knowing she's terrified of her own father breaks me.

"No sweetie, daddy loves us," I lie. "I think he's just feeling unwell at the minute."

"That big man hurt Ryder."

"He did, I'm sure Ryder is fine though, he's really big and strong."

There's alight tap on the door, followed by the turning of the key and I push to sit up, praying it isn't Finn. Mary enters pushing a trolly. She glances up and her eyes fix on Harlee. "Sorry I didn't realise there was a child."

"This is Harlee," I tell her.

"I'll go grocery shopping later today. I'll bring you a pen and paper to write a list of what she likes."

"I'm allergic to fish," says Harlee, quietly.

"I'll make sure that you don't have any fish, Harlee," she says with a smile. It's the first one she's cracked and it lights up her face.

"Is Finn around this morning?" I ask.

"Yes, he said he'd be up after breakfast." She leaves and I head over to the trolley which is laden with food. I scoop some fresh chopped food into a bowl and give it to Harlee.

"I can eat in bed?" she asks, smiling.

I nod. "Yes. I don't even care if you get it on the sheets."

I watch as she scoffs down the fruit, followed by toast and then yoghurt. At least if she's eating, she's not too traumatised. I, on the other hand, can't touch a thing. I'm sick to my stomach with worry and stress, and all I can think about is how I'm going to get out of this mess.

Twenty minutes later, Finn appears looking fresh and relaxed. I want to punch him in his smug face as he takes a seat by the window. "Good morning my beautiful princesses. Did you sleep well?"

Harlee snuggles into my back, hiding from his sight. He narrows his eyes, "Harlee why are you hiding from me?"

"Are you for real?" I snap. "You scared her last night, she's terrified of her own father."

"Harlee, that was all mummy's fault," he says in a clipped tone. "She broke daddy's rules and I had every right to be angry about that."

"Don't you dare blame this on me," I hiss, feeling Harlee tense. I take a deep, calming breath. "I'd rather not talk about this in front of her."

Finn stands gracefully, going over to the bedside cabinet and taking out an iPad and headphones. He hands it to Harlee who grabs it gratefully, looking at me for permission. I nod, taking it from her briefly to put on her favourite cartoon. Once she's settled, he fixes me with a glare. "No more excuses." I picture diving at him, punching him over and over, wondering if Harlee is distracted enough not to notice me lose my shit. Instead I rolled my eyes in that way I know pisses him off.

"Now, rules," he continues with a smirk. "Number one, you can't leave this house. There are guards everywhere, camera's everywhere and windows and doors will be kept locked. If you leave, the guards are instructed to shoot."

I laugh, wondering if he realises how stupid he sounds. "Shoot me? Like with an actual fucking gun, Finn. Do you realise how crazy this all sounds. This isn't a movie, we aren't in America where guns are carried. What kind of world are you living in where you think this is okay?"

"My world," he says with confidence.

I arch a brow. "Your world? Fine. Okay. So if I was to step outside with your five-year-old daughter in my arms, you're telling me your men will kill us?"

"Run outside with her and find out, Neve. I dare you."

I pinch the bridge of my nose. "I feel like I've woken in a different world. Why are you doing this to us, Finn?"

"You're my girls and you belong to me."

"So it's about power and possession. I don't belong to anyone. Not Ryder and certainly not you. You can't own another person, Finn, it's mental. All of this is mental."

"Of all the men in this fucking world you had to fall for that piece of shit. Just like fucking Alice! You have been fucking my enemy. He controls you and you let him so yes, he thinks he owns you, owns what's mine. You gave me no choice but to take you back."

I startle at the Alice comment, he's never mentioned her to me and it sounded so personal. "Ryder doesn't control me..."

"Since we broke up, Neve, we've spoken every single night. He comes a long and that stops. Of course he's controlled you, you're just too stupid to see it."

"Ryder was right, Finn, my life is none of your business. You left us. After that, you only had the right to ask about our daughter."

"Rule two," he continued, ignoring her comment, "If you attempt to break rule number one then Harlee will suffer."

I jump to my feet and he does the same, meeting me chest to chest. "Don't you dare threaten my daughter," I hiss.

Finn grins, running a finger down my cheek, using enough pressure to hurt. "She's our daughter, Neve."

I take a breath and a step back. If I goad him to hurt me, it leaves me weak and I have to be strong for Harlee. I have to get us out of here. I give him a pleading look, "Why can't you just let us go, Finn, and get on with your life?"

"I'll leave the iPad with you for Harlee, there's no internet, the movies are pre-downloaded so don't even think about trying to contact anyone on the outside. The sooner you accept this life the better. I'll leave the door unlocked so you can explore but remember what I said."

He leaves, keeping the door open a jar. I go over to the window and stare down at the high wall surrounding us. There's no way I can jump that, especially with a five-year old. And Finn wasn't lying, there are men walking around the grounds, some even have dogs. I sigh out loud. *Fuck.*

Chapter Sixteen

Ryder

I wake with a start and glance around. My head still aches bad and it takes me a second to focus. There's an irritating beeping sound and I glance to my left to see a machine.

Griff appears, placing a hand on my chest. "Take it easy, pres."

"Where the hell am I?" I growl, feeling irritated.

"Hospital. We found you at Neve's place passed out on the bed. You've had a bleed on the brain."

I frown, letting his words process. I remember everything up to calling Griff for help. "How long have I been here?"

"Three days. How are you feeling?"

"Like shit. Three days in here when I should have been looking for Neve and Harlee."

I push to sit up but he stops me again. "Relax," he orders. "We're on it. Finn was asking for security a couple of days ago. We've put a man on the inside. He's not wherever Finn is keeping Neve, only his inside circle are there. But there is an event happening tonight and he thinks Neve might be there."

"Can trust this guy? Who is he?" I'm not used to being out of touch or not in control of everything. The fact I've been out of it for three days makes my guilt ten times worse. She needs me and I'm stuck here.

"Yeah, he's an ex-copper, a good guy and a good friend of mine. I wouldn't have put him on it if I wasn't one hundred percent sure I could trust him. Let me call for the doctor."

"Don't bother, I'm going home." I sit up and begin pulling the wires off my chest.

"Pres that's not a good idea. The bleeds stopped but one knock and who knows. You need rest and time to heal."

"I am not lying in bed while my old lady is held up fuck knows where, going through fuck knows what. I want her back and I want that fucker dead."

Griff sighs, "I'll speak to the doctor but he's gonna advise against it."

"I don't give a crap, do whatever it takes to get me out of here."

Neve

Three days, we've been here for three damn days with no sign of the mc and not a single chance to escape this hell. All kinds of scenarios have filled my head these last few days, one being that Ryder hasn't made it. That breaks my heart. And the other being that the mc have found him and think I've done it and gone on the run.

"Mary do you like working here?" I ask, peeling a potato.

"Neve, you know we can't talk about things like that. If Finnegan overheard, he'd be mad." It's another one of Finn's stupid rules. All staff have been warned not to befriend me. He's already guessed that I'd try that first. If the staff feel sorry for me, they might help me leave. Mary gives me a sympathetic smile. "I've worked here a long time. Since Finnegan was a small boy."

"You knew his parents?" I ask, feeling relieved that she hasn't chose to work for Finn but has perhaps done it more out of obligation.

"That's enough chit chat, chop those potatoes."

"I didn't know Finns parents. When we married, they weren't at the wedding."

"They died. A long time ago now."

"Oh, Finn didn't tell me that. Do you have children?"

"Miss Lawrence, please," she mutters uncomfortably.

"Sorry, I'm just lonely." I haven't seen Finn for days, which isn't a bad thing. But it also means that adult conversation is scarce and I'm losing my mind. "Can I do anything else to help?" I'm not supposed to help and Mary took some convincing yesterday when I insisted. Doing everyday things helps me to keep focussed.

The front door opens then slams and Finn is heard yelling in what I assume is his mobile. Mary looks at me in alarm and I rush towards the lounge, throwing myself onto the couch before he spots me. I grab a magazine and pretend I'm concentrating.

"What do you mean it went wrong. Somebody had to have tipped them off because the police don't randomly show up at the fucking docks in the middle of the night. I want a name." He enters the living room just as he's shoving his mobile back into his pocket. "Where's Harlee?"

"Having a nap. She isn't feeling well."

"Stand," he growls. I do so immediately. His eyes have that darkness that means I shouldn't test his patience. He hasn't touched me so far, in fact, it feels like he's avoiding me which has been nice. "Your boyfriend is out of hospital," he says, taking my hand and tugging me towards him. "I've sent him some flowers to wish him a speedy recovery." I hold my breath to hide the relief I feel at hearing that Ryder is alive.

Finn slides his hand around my waist, "It's been too long since I've held you," he whispers and for a split second, I see the old Finn. The one that fooled me into thinking he was a nice guy. I allow him to pull me close and press his nose into my hair and taking a deep inhale. I brush my hand over his jacket, feeling his mobile phone sticking out of the pocket and I carefully slide it free and hold it tightly. As he releases me, I stuff it in my back pocket and smile awkwardly.

"I thought you were avoiding me," I say lightly, even though inside I'm sick with nerves. If he realises it's gone, he'll lose his mind.

"I've been busy with work. Let's have dinner this evening, we can catch up and talk about what happens next."

I give a stiff nod and he turns, marching towards his office. I wait for him to go out of sight before running for the stairs, taking them two at a time. My foot hits the top one and I hear him running up behind me. "You stupid little bitch," he roars.

I run along the landing but he catches me, shoving me into the wall. "Finn," I cry, "I just needed to check Harlee's symptoms. I'm worried about her."

Finn holds out his hand and I reluctantly place the mobile in it. He tucks it away. He reaches behind me to turn the handle to another room and I fall back onto my backside and begin to crawl backwards to put some distance between us. He smirks, matching each move back with a step forward, "I thought we'd turned a corner, Neve. You've behaved so well."

"Fuck you," I hiss angrily. "Fuck you and your stupid bullshit rules."

He sniggers, like me retaliating is exactly what he wants. He swoops down, grabbing my arm and slamming his free fist into my face. The blows keep coming. Each one harder than the last. Some on my face and head, others in my stomach. I close my eyes, trying to block out his angry words and heavy fists. I picture a beach and Harlee is splashing in the water, her giggle infectious. An arm is wrapped around me and I turn to look in Ryder's kind eye. *Fuck*, what I'd give to see them right now for real.

I feel myself being lifted. The smell doesn't belong to Finn, I hate his spicy scent. This one smelt of alcohol and sweat. I prize one eye open, the other refuses and I assume it's swollen shut. The man holding me is large. His head is large and his hands are even larger, and he carries me down the stairs with little effort like I weigh nothing. He goes through the kitchen and towards that door that's always kept locked. I don't have any energy to argue and I spot Mary holding the door open for us to go inside and as we pass, she keeps her head lowered.

We descend the stone steps and as we get lower, the air changes to cold and damp. There are no windows and the only light is from a dim bulb hanging in the centre. I glance around and spot three dirty mattresses on the ground. The man deposits me on the nearest one, and pain radiates through my body. I clutch my ribs, wincing. "Wait," I whisper, my voice cracking. "What about Harlee?" He doesn't bother to look back, instead taking the stairs two at a time and slamming the door closed.

I ease myself into a sitting position and look around the cellar. Apart from the mattresses, there's not much else here. There's a black bucket in the corner with another dim light above it, which I assume will be my toilet for however long I'm here. I wrap my arms around myself, trying to keep warm and the damp surrounds me. I take a blanket that's folded neatly on the end of the mattress and bring it to my nose, and sniff, screwing my nose up in disgust. It smells damp but I pull it around me anyway. I lie back and close my eyes, taking my mind back to the day I met Finn, remembering how charming he was.

"I'm Finnegan, your husband to be," he'd announced confidently. I'd laughed at the corny chat up line, but I let him kiss my hand anyway, it wasn't often a man in London took your hand to kiss the back of it.

"Neve," I'd replied shyly. I wasn't usually so shy, but this man was dressed in an expensive suit, he was handsome, and he was staring directly into my eyes with a piercing, panty melting look.

"Neve, I like it. Let me buy you a drink and then we'll make plans for our wedding."

He'd led me to the bar, purchased a bottle of Champagne and told the bartender that they were celebrating their engagement. I'd blushed, he was so forward and confident and it turned me on. I'd thought it odd that he didn't have friends with him, just big burly looking men that he referred to as security. But Mya had encouraged me to approach the guy, telling me to accept a drink and enjoy being spoilt by an obviously rich man, neither of us suspected anything odd, but then we'd been swept up in the world-wide Christian Grey hype, and were all on the lookout for rich billionaire boyfriends.

Four months later, he was true to his word, we got married. It was a fairy-tale that I hadn't really been expecting. I was still young, and the thought of marriage scared me but everyone around me convinced me I was lucky.

The sex between us was constant, a little too much to be honest but I accepted that Finn had a higher sex drive and he had particular tastes. His violence in the bedroom would be contained there, and afterwards he was like the Finn I'd first met, charming and sweet. It was a shock to me when I fell pregnant, it was unplanned, but I felt happy, after all, most of our relationship had been a whirl wind and this was natural progression. Finn didn't see it like that. He was furious and it was the first time in our short relationship that he brought violence outside of the bedroom. He then disappeared for weeks. When he returned, he had become distant and practically ignored me. I was sure by then he'd met someone else, he'd stopped having sex with me and avoided me like I was diseased. Eventually he told me I had to leave, he didn't want me or the baby. I left that night. That was that, and he seemed fine with it. And honestly, I was relieved, the few weeks we'd spent apart gave me clarity and I saw the relationship for what it was. If he'd hit me once, then he'd do it again and again.

Of course, it wasn't that simple. Finn would turn up unannounced at my house. He'd call all the time and the night time calls became a thing with him flying off the handle if I didn't pick up. I put up with it for a quiet life and I found that if I answered his calls, he didn't pop and see me as much, and so it became a habit, answer his calls, answer his questions and then he'd leave me alone.

The sound of the lock wakes me and I sit up. I don't know how long I've been here and without daylight, I can't even guess.

Footsteps descend and the large man appears again. I can just make out a pair of legs dangling over his arms. I push myself back into the corner and watch him suspiciously as he approaches. He dumps the female on the next mattress without looking in my direction.

"Where's Finn, I want to speak with Finn?" I demand. He doesn't respond, simply leaves without a word. I wait for the lock to click in place before scrambling over to the woman. She's naked and covered in bruises, so I slip out of my shirt and place it over her head, wrestling it down her slim frame. I pull her onto her side, listening carefully to her shallow breaths as I put her into the recovery position.

Ryder

I sit back in my chair and wait for the brother's to take a seat around the large table. I'd called church the second I got back to the club. We need to all be on the same page when it comes to taking down Finn fucking Lawerence.

I bang the gavel on the table to get everyone's attention. The sound sends a radiating pain through my skull but I ignore it, whatever pain I'm in, is probably a lot less that Neve's right now.

I throw the dead bunch of flowers onto the table and then men stare at them. "A get well present from the bastard himself," I snap, "We staked out a few of Finn's known businesses last night. Cal, fill us in."

"We spent the night watching the docks where Finn brings his drugs in. All quiet, his lock up wasn't manned and so we knocked on, couldn't hear anything and we eventually managed to break in, but it was empty. We think he's moved bases because we'd hit it the boat last week. He also runs with the Irish and so we checked their spot out but again nothing untoward."

"Okay, Knox?" I ask, moving on.

"Same boss, nothing. We watched his house in central London. He had a party there which he attended with a blond female. By the end of the night it had turned to a swinger's party, sex everywhere, including the garden. He left before that started but he was alone. We followed him to his bar on Canal Street," Knox looked down at his notes, "Cantrell's. An hour after he went inside some Italian looking guys went in, but we couldn't get in without being obvious. They left two hours later, and we followed him back to his house where the party had finished. He's acting normal boss, with no sign of Neve or the kid."

I slam my hands on the table in frustration, the pain getting worse in my head. "I need to meet with him."

"It's not a good idea, Pres," Griff advises, "It's what he wants and you're in no fit state to get into a fight with him. Besides, I have some news. I heard from my guy on the inside. He's been put on security for a few of Finn's sex parties, they're always underground, with only certain members allowed. Mainly rich men. Anyway, he's at another warehouse tonight. It's all hush hush but he thinks that girls are being sold there. He'd heard from a few of Finn's men that Finn used his boat to bring in foreign girls. He's apparently promising them a good life and once they're here, he has them trained to be submissive. If my man confirms all this tonight, he can pass it on to the force as intelligence."

I sit straighter, "The cops won't do shit. He's untouchable and always has been. Half those rich bastards will be judges or cops themselves," I spit angrily. "I'm screwed either way. I can't kill the fucker in case he's the only one that knows where Neve is." I rub my hands over my tired face. "What if he's sold Neve?" And for the first time, I feel completely useless.

"I doubt it. He's choosing foreign girls that can't talk to ask for help, and even if they could, why would they when they're here illegally? They're more scared of our authorities than they are of criminals like Finn, he will have told them horror stories of what will happen to them if they run," says Griff.

I take a deep breath and nod in agreement. It makes sense. And I can't imagine Neve keeping quite or complying without too much of a fuss. "I'm gonna contact the Italians and see if we can do a better deal that Finn. They'll be asking questions about his ability to provide the guns and drugs after us hitting his boat twice. Let's strike now." The guys nod in agreement and I bang the gavel down, signalling the end of our meeting.

I head for the office and call Benedetto Ricci's mobile. He answers straight away, his tone guarded, after all, I've already turned down two deals previously from the Italians. "Ethan Ryder Fenton," he drawls in his Italian accent, "To what do I owe this pleasure?"

"Benedetto, how are you?"

"All good, is there a problem?"

"No, no problem. I wanted to arrange a meet with you."

There's a long pause. "About?" he eventually asks.

"Business. I hear that Finnegan Lawrence isn't as reliable as he once promised."

"Where did you hear that, Ryder? Your source is wrong." Trust the Italians to not want to lose face and admit they've made a bad choice.

"I don't think so Ben, to have his boat hit once is concerning, but twice, well..." I trail off.

"Twice?" Ben repeats. Clearly this is the first he's heard about it. Finn must have made up some bullshit to delay his delivery.

"Yes, his boats are unguarded and he's spending more time dealing in sex slaves than guns. We all know that slavery is a mugs game, you'd think our hot shot lawyer friend would also know this. You have younger sisters, Ben, you're a smart man, you know women are worth their weight in gold. They shouldn't be treated in such a bad way."

"Where have you heard all of this?" Benedetto's voice is angry, and I smile to myself.

"Meet me and we'll talk properly. Maybe I can offer you a better deal?"

"Fine, come to Nico's this evening at ten thirty."

I disconnect as Griff enters the office. "We're meeting the Italian's at Nico's tonight. Let's come up with a deal he won't refuse."

Chapter Seventeen

Neve

I have spent hours keeping the woman warm. She shivers uncontrollably even though I'm wrapped around her with all three blankets too. I stroke her hair again and she stirs. Relief floods me, I was beginning to give up hope. She opens her eyes and they dart around in sheer panic. I smile kindly, "It's okay," I whisper, "You're going to be okay. I'm Neve."

"Neve," she repeats, her voice croaky. "I Malia." I realise she's not from England and my heart sinks. This poor woman isn't going to understand anything I say and she's probably terrified.

"How did you get here?" I ask and she looks at me blankly. I put my arms out like an aeroplane, "You fly?" I ask. "Boat?" I add, moving my hand up and down like it's going over water. I sigh heavily.

"Boat," she repeats, smiling and I nod.

"Yes, boat, on water?" She nods.

"Family?" I ask hopefully.

This time she shakes her head sadly. "Better life," she says, nodding. "I here for better life."

"With Finn. Finnegan?" I ask. She stares blankly again but the sound of the lock opening grabs our attention and she pushes back against me like she's trying to hide.

Mary pops a tray on the top step and I dive up, rushing up the steps. "Mary, wait," I gasp desperately. She hesitates. "It she okay, is Harlee okay?" I cry.

Mary glances back over her shoulder and turns back to Neve. "She's fine. I'm looking after her well," she whispers, smiling.

"Is Finn there, please ask him to come, I'll do whatever he wants."

"I haven't seen him in a few days. Harlee is fine. I promise I'll take care of her." I frown, her words sound so final.

"Mary, what do you mean?"

She steps back and closes the door. I bang my fists against it, yelling Finn's name over and over until my voice is hoarse.

Malia approaches me cautiously, and I realise I must look crazy behaving like this, but I feel so helpless.

On the tray is two bottles of water, four pain killers and two cheese sandwiches. Malia carries the tray down the steps and I follow. We sit in silence eating, and I think over ideas on how to get Finn's attention.

A few more hours have passed since we ate and we've both slept for most of it. It's only the sound of the lock that gets us stirring. Footsteps descend and I recognise his shiny shoes right away. "Wake up Princess, I hear you've been begging for me." I sit up and he comes to a stop, looking at me with disgust. "Let's get you cleaned up."

"I can leave?" I ask, hardly believing it.

"I need your services for a while."

"What about Malia?" I ask as he holds out a hand.

I stand and take it. "She'll be fine."

Ryder

"It's a good deal," mused Benedetto, his fingers rubbing his goatee.

"A very good deal. We're much more reliable than Finn, that's why you came to us months ago," says Griff. "I'm sure you were just as sickened as us to hear about his recent dealings in sex slaves."

"I came to you months ago and you turned me down. I'm meeting with Finn later this evening. I'll discuss these rumours with him."

"Meeting Finn, where?" I ask.

Ben eyes me suspiciously and Griff leans forward. "He's taken Ryders old lady," he says and I glare at him. "We've been trying to track her down."

"I've never seen him with a woman. But this does explain your enthusiasm to ruin him," says Ben.

"We're being honest with you, Ben, that's how we do business. We don't hide shit and we don't lie," says Griff.

"That's a good quality, I like that. Maybe we can discuss this offer further in the morning once I've straightened things with Finn? I'll let you know if I see your old lady."

He stands and we shake hands, signalling the end of our meeting.

"We're gonna lose out on that deal, we'll hardly make anything from it," mutters Griff.

"If it's what we have to do to ruin that fuck, then we'll do it. I'll cover any loss to the club," I tell him.

"Man, we're playing a dangerous game. What if he gets desperate and hurts Neve or worse, sells Harlee.""Shut the fuck up, Griff. You're not helping."

"I'm here to speak the truth man, you asked that of me. You wanted me to be the eyes and ears when you weren't thinking straight and so here I am. I asked you not to make this deal, yet I'm here supporting you. I said this might blow up in our faces, yet we're still here."

I sigh heavily, he's right, he thinks clearly when I can't and I know saving Neve is taking over my sanity. "You told him the truth about Neve," I mutter.

"Because he's the kind of man that appreciates honesty. He wouldn't have fallen for that deal knowing you're making a fucking loss."

Finn hands me a silver dress. It glitters in the bathroom lights and I snatch it angrily. "You promised I could see Harlee," I snap.

He pulls the towel from my body and I do my best to cover myself with the dress. He pulls that too, leaving me exposed. He makes a grab for my breast and I recoil, folding my arms to cover that area. He sniggers, "You need to play a role this evening. I have the police chief meeting us for dinner."

I feel a glimmer of hope but it's soon snatched away when he grabs me to him, turning me to face the mirror. He runs his hands over my chest, batting my hands away from my breasts. He cups them, smirking at my reflection in the mirror. "I know what you're thinking. That this could be your chance to escape, to get help. Well if you want to see Harlee again, you'll play by my rules."

"I can't believe you'd stoop so low as to threaten your own daughter."

He grins wider. "As long as I have you, I don't care about anything or anyone else." My heart breaks a little more at his disregard for our daughter. "You know, your boyfriend hasn't been in touch. Do you think he's given up?"

"No."

He smirks, burying his face into my neck and nipping the skin. I shudder with repulsion. "Maybe he doesn't care like you thought."

"Why are we having dinner with the chief of police?" I ask, changing the subject because the thought of Ryder giving up on us, makes me sick to my stomach.

"A precaution. Questions will be asked and when..." he paused and smiled, "Sorry, if Ryder does decide to get desperate and report you missing, I want the police to be able to shut him down. Always one step ahead Princess. Now get dressed." He steps away and I sag in relief, grabbing the dress from him and slipping it on under his watchful eye. "Your role tonight will be the doting wife. Smile in all the right places, be attentive to me and act like I am your world."

"And if I don't you'll hurt our little girl?" I snap. "Where is she exactly?"

"She's with Mary," he replies. At least that's something. I don't think Mary would hurt her, she seemed quite taken with her. "Mary lost her child, I think it was a girl, new-born. She was devastated and never went on to try again. She'll make a good mother one day." He sees the way I stiffen and sighs, "Maybe I can give her what she's always wanted. Harlee will forget about you soon enough and she can have a loving mother."

I slap him. It's hard and stings my hand instantly. He wastes no time reacting, grabbing me by the throat and slamming me hard into the mirror. I grin, glad I've hurt him too as the red mark appears on his cheek. "Fuck you, you prick," I hiss through gritted teeth. "I hope you fucking die a painfully long death."

He sneers, "I love it when you fight me, Neve, it makes life interesting from that boring little bitch you'd become." He presses his erection into my thigh and I fight myself not to vomit as he grabs the hem of my dress and begins to shove it up.

"No," I snap, shoving his hands away. "No fucking chance."

"Keep fighting me, Princess, it makes it sweeter when I finally get inside you and win."

He roughly shoves his hand between my legs and I cry out in anger. I don't want to give him a fight but there is no fucking way he's forcing me to have sex with him.

There's bang on the door and Finn stills. "What?"

"Boss, the car is ready, we need to leave on time."

Finn laughs, resting his head against my forehead, our breathing short and heavy. "We'll have to pick this up later, princess."

The restaurant is crowded and the smell of cooked garlic makes my stomach growl in hunger. The waiter leads us to a table by the window, pulling out my seat for me to lower into. The view of the Thames relaxes me slightly. Just being out of that house is a good feeling. The waiter returns seconds later with a couple, the man older with a ruddy complexion and the woman thin with pointed features. She gives a stern look my way as she's seated and I instantly get the feeling I won't like her.

"Charles, it's so good to see you. And this must be Helen, how lovely to finally meet you." Finn oozes charm, kissing Helen's hand just like he had done to me all those years ago. "This is my wife, Neve."

We all shake hands before sitting back down. Finn places his hand on my knee and gives it a rough squeeze. "I thought you were separated," asks Charles.

"We were, but you can't fight love. For all my sins, Neve loves me and I love her. We're giving our marriage a second chance."

"That's good to hear. So many people give up too easily, especially you young ones."

"Yes, Harlee is our pride and joy. We want her to be happy."

I struggle to concentrate on any of the conversation because my mind is consumed with food. I'm so hungry and the divine smells are making it impossible to think of anything else. A waitress places a bowl in front of me and I almost whoop for joy.

"Thank you," I say politely.

I polish off the soup before everyone else at the table, not having the energy to be worried how that makes me look. The next course is steak and salad, and it goes just as quickly as the soup. The chief shoots me a quizzical look on more than one occasion, but I simply smile. Once I'm finished, I lay my white cloth napkin over the steak knife and tune in to their conversation, waiting for them all to be occupied before sliding it onto my lap and then dropping it into my clutch on the floor.

We say our goodbyes after coffee and cheese. I managed a few more mouthfuls but had to give up when my stomach aches in protest. Sickness bubbles away inside as I slide into the waiting car, itching for my bed so I can slip into a food coma.

Finn slides in beside me and pushes the button to raise the divide between us and the driver.

"Well done. I'll perhaps let Harlee see you for two minutes tomorrow."

I frown, sitting up straighter. "Tomorrow? But you said tonight."

"It's extremely late. Harlee will be asleep."

My heart squeezes with disappointment. "Please, let me just look at her. I won't wake her."

"Don't be a drama queen, Neve. I prefer you as a fighter." He pauses before adding, "Besides, it depends how well you perform when we get home."

"What do you mean?" I ask cautiously.

"I'm going to send lover boy a video, I'm sure he's missing you."

"Don't be ridiculous, he's not looking so leave him be."

Finn laughs, "He's going to cause me problems and I'd rather know when that's going to happen. All this waiting around is boring."

I slip my hand into the clutch bag and grip the knife handle. "You'll want me to fight?"

He smirks. "Of course. I want him to hear you begging for your life, princess. Let's spring him into action."

"I'd rather die," I say coldly and he glances at me. "I won't fight on camera or any other time," I spit.

He arches a brow, "Is that right. Let's see." He grabs my dress, yanking it hard enough to rip up the centre.

I kick out and he laughs, "You can't help it. It's instinct to survive."

"It's instinct to keep you the fuck away from me," I yell as he pulls my legs apart and kneels between them.

"Baby, why are you pretending you don't want this as much as me? We fight, we fuck, it's what we like."

"It's what you like," I hiss, kicking out again. "I've never enjoyed a second in the bedroom with you."

He runs his hands up my thighs, lowering his head to my stomach and licking the skin there. "I'm going to fuck you like you deserve," he growls, gripping my ankle and lifting my leg over his shoulder. "Hard, fast and painful."

I laugh and it throws him off guard, he raises his head right as I pull my hand from my clutch and raise the knife. I slam it into his shoulder and he cries out in pain. I withdraw it and try again, this time missing as he shuffles back from me. I lean forward, slashing around until I make contact, not caring where I hit, as long as I do. "You asked for a fight," I scream, "So fucking fight me." He tries to grab my wrists but I'm too frantic in my movement.

He pushes up onto his knees and lays over me, eventually pinning my arms to my sides. He headbutts me hard and I feel my nose spray out. "Drop it," he hisses, squeezing my wrist tightly until I release the blade. He grabs it, and falls back onto the seat, gripping his shoulder.

"Die," I whisper desperately as his breaths come out loud and rattling. "Please just fucking die." His eyes reach mine and I smirk. "that'll be the only time you hear me beg," I spit.

The car stops and the door is pulled open. The driver stares back and forth between us, taking in Finn's blood-stained shirt and my ripped dress. He reaches into the car, grabbing my arm and dragging me out. I land on my knees, trying desperately to scramble to my feet. He pulls me up the steps and the big man comes into view. I begin to back away, shaking my head in panic. "No," I whisper, "no, no, no." He grabs me as the driver tells him that the 'boss' is hurt.

The door to the cellar is opened and I'm thrown in like a rag doll. Rolling down the stairs until I land in a heap at the bottom. He slams the door and locks it.

Malia rushes over and I wince as she tries to help me sit. I shake my head, choosing to crawl over to my mattress because walking is too painful. I'm dizzy from the blow to my face and every limb aches. As I drag myself over the cold floor, I heave, spilling the contents of dinner onto the concrete. I sob, angry that I've lost the fullness from my stomach.

As I lay on my mattress, I notice the other is now occupied. Malia goes to her and lies behind her, stroking her hair just like I'd done to her. I smile to myself, closing my eyes and letting the darkness take me.

Chapter Eighteen

Ryder

It was early, or late, depending on how you wanted to look at it. I groan, rolling onto my side and opening my eyes. I frown in confusion, and as I push to sit up, I fall from the bed, landing with an humph. Sassy peers over the edge, smirking, "Morning."

"What are you doing here?" I ask, pushing to my knees, relieved when I see she's fully clothed.

"You asked me to stay with you, can't you remember?" she asks.

I shake my head trying to search my memories from last night. The only clear one was the empty bottle of whiskey I'd consumed alone. "I dropped by last night to check on you, I've been worried."

"Why were you worried?" I ask, standing. I haven't told her anything about Neve or Harlee.

"I saw Bear's old lady in town, she mentioned you've been having a rough time. Plus you haven't been to see Alfie and you've dodged my calls."

"I told you I've been busy."

"You texted me one time," she says, "So I was worried. And it looks like I was right to be, you were in such a state when I got here."

"Did I ask you to stay in my bed?" I query, because my mind is so full of Neve, I find it impossible to believe.

"You got a little upset when I put you to bed."

"I got upset?" I repeat, confused. "That doesn't sound like me."

"Don't be embarrassed, we all crack at some time or another. Besides, it's just me, we don't have to hide stuff from each other."

I grunt and head off for a shower, hoping she takes the hint and leaves. But when I return she's still sprawled out on the bed looking through her mobile. "You're still here?"

"I was thinking that we could go and collect Alfie, and then spend the day together?"

"I have shit to do Sass, maybe another time. I'd love to see Alfie though, how would you feel about me collecting him at a set time each weekend and having him for a couple of hours?" It was an idea I was going to put to her before everything went south with Neve. But now seems like as good a time as any.

She narrows her eyes. "He doesn't know you, Ryder. We should take it slow and visit together as a family unit. He needs to trust you and so do I."

"But we aren't a family unit, Sass. He needs to see us getting along, I agree, but not together or he'll get confused."

"I've got a better idea. Why don't I collect him and bring him back here later this afternoon? You can spend some time with him, and I'll just be around?"

I think over her offer, it's the best I'm likely to get so I reluctantly nod and she grins, throwing the sheets back and standing. "Great, I'll just grab a shower and then I'll be on my way."

When she returns a few minutes later wrapped in a towel, I stand. I feel uncomfortable and I know how bad this would look should anyone come barging in. The last thing I need is the gossip wheels turning. Neve would never understand.

I take my keys and phone from the side. "I'll leave you to it," I say.

She laughs, unwrapping her towel from her naked body and using it to rub her hair. "Don't tell me you're shy, Ryder. God, you used to order me to walk around you naked, and now you can't even look at me. I'm the mother of your child for goodness sake."

I glue my eyes to the floor. She's right, there was a time when I would make her walk around the room naked just so I could have access to her any time I wanted. I risk a quick glance up, taking in her new body. It had changed over the years, her breasts were fuller and her thighs thicker, it gave her a sexy edge. Squeezing my keys hard in my palm I race for the door. The sound of Sassy giggling as I leave rings out. It would be easier to go back there, secure my place in Alfie's life and live like a family, but I love Neve too much to fuck it all up. She's my future. Her, Harlee and Alfie.

"Pres, where the hell have you been. I've been calling you." Griff looks pissed as he marches towards me.

"Sorry, slept in, bad hangover."

"Tell me about it. You were wasted last night."

"Am I not allowed to drink in my own damn club?" I growl and Griff holds his hands up in surrender.

"Sorry. Benedetto's been in touch. He couldn't get hold of Finn last night and then he saw some photo's on the Chief of Police's social media account, he sent them to me," says Griff pulling out his mobile. I raise a surprised brow and Griff laughs, "I know, tell me about it, the Chief having a social media account. Apparently, it's to ensure good relations with the public."

He pushes his mobile under my nose, showing a photograph of Finn with the Chief, the caption reads, *'Working together with local business owners.'*

"So," I say, shrugging. Griff grins and zooms in on the picture. It shows a reflection in the glass window, I can just make out the image of Neve and my whole world stops spinning for a second. Relief floods me and Griff pats me on the back. "He has her still, and she's alive. That's the confirmation you needed."

"But they're out together. With the chief. Is she there by choice?" Suddenly doubts flood my mind. What if she's gone back to Finn of her own free will and the whole abduction thing is a disguise so that Ryder doesn't follow her?

"Brother, you're over thinking. They wouldn't go to all that trouble. He's holding her somewhere and this was a stage for him to cover his arse. So, while you were sleeping off your hangover, I called the chief, told him that I'd been having an affair with the girl in that picture and so I needed to know who she was to Finn. Finn told him that they were making a go of their marriage, but the Chief said she was quiet and withdrawn. She had faded bruises and she looked unwell, like she hadn't eaten in days. He asked if that shit was my fault or Finn's, cheeky fucker."

"Fuck, I just need her back, Griff. I can't function without her. Should we tell the chief she's been taken?"

Griff shakes his head, "We all know he's a bent mother fucker, we'll be in his debt and who knows what shit he'll have us doing. Let's leave him as a last resort. My guy got in touch, he's at another warehouse tonight but this time he's inside. He's one hundred percent sure that they are auctioning women off."

"Let's hope he doesn't decide to auction off Neve!"

"And risk the chief asking questions, it wouldn't happen."

Adelina, the new woman in the cellar, is also not from England. But she speaks some English which makes communication so much better between us all. We sit crossed legged on the bed listening to how she left her home in Syria some weeks ago to come here and clean houses for rich people. She was sold a dream that would see her and her parents much better off financially. But when she got here, she realised she'd entered a nightmare.

"A man met me, he took me to hotel. Two men there waiting, it felt not right," she says, her English broken in places. "I scared. I try to run but I get caught and beaten and . . . and hurt, then I bring here!" I sit patiently whilst they speak in their own language.

I feel sick knowing this is all down to Finn. I gave him a child and now I'm tied to him forever. I knew deep down when I met him I should have been more cautious, should have asked more questions but everything was so rushed and I didn't have time to think too deeply about where all his money came from or why he was always buying nice gifts whenever I questioned him.

"We escape, Malia have plan," smiles Adelina.

I shake my head, "We can't, there are too many guards out there with big dogs and guns. They'll kill us." Adelina recounts that to Malia and they both look crestfallen.

"We think of other plan?" Adelina suggests.

I nod in agreement, not sure what we could possibly come up with but not wanting to crush them any further.

The door opens and we break apart, waiting to see who descends the stairs. The times it's a large man with a protruding stomach hanging over his tight belt. His cheeks are ruddy and red, and he seemed short of breath by the time he reaches the bottom step. Two men follow, holding guns by their sides and wearing an earpiece. For a second, I think they're here to help and I get to my feet. It's soon diminished as the man sneers, "Just three, is Finnegan trying to make me look stupid?"

A man on the steps puts his mobile to his ear while the fat man circles me, eyeing my body in the ripped dress. He seems unconcerned by the dried blood on my face or across my legs. He then reaches for Malia, tugging her to stand and circling her. I focus back to the man on the phone, realising he's talking to Finn, which means I didn't manage to kill the fucker. "Get here now!" he orders, before disconnecting.

I turn to the sound of Malia sobbing, watching as the man runs a finger along her collar bone. "Is he coming?"

"On his way, Sir."

"This one is too skinny," he grumbles, turning away from Malia and reaching for Adelina. "But this one, umm, I like this one. Name?"

"Adelina," she whispers.

"I like that name, pity you won't get to keep it." He grips her shirt between his pudgy hands and tugs hard until it rips and the buttons fly off. Adelina flinches, folding her arms to cover herself.

"Hey," I yell angrily, "Don't do that, leave her alone." I push myself between them.

"You're English," he smirks. "Interesting."

"Fuck you," I spit and he slaps me across the face so hard, I fall to the ground.

"Maybe this one would be more entertaining," he says, and the two other men laugh.

Finn runs down the steps, looking harassed. His eyes darted between me and the man. "Mr Sharp, I wasn't expecting you until this evening."

"Clearly, three girls, Finnegan, three?" The man moves towards Finn, "How can I put on a show with just three women?"

"Erm, actually two. She's not a part of this," says Finn, nodding his head towards me.

"Oh, she is, unless you can get me at least three more then she is very much a part of this. You have..." the man looks at his large gold watch and smiles, "Three hours."

Ryder

I look down at the little boy squashed into my side as he watches television, and smile. I should feel much happier but this memory is overshadowed by the fact I'm missing Neve and all I can think about is ways to get to her.

Alfie snuggles closer. "I think he's getting sleepy," says Sassy.

"Oh right, do you need a ride home?" I ask.

"Actually, why don't I..."

She's interrupted when Griff storms into the room. "Pres, we need to talk now." I extract my arm from around my son and follow him to the office. "We don't have time to call church. My guy just rang, he's been given the location in advance. That never happens but apparently somethings spooked Finn and he's acting all crazy. Word got around that his wife stabbed him. He's been in hospital."

"Shit. I hope he didn't hurt her," I mutter. "I feel so fucking useless just waiting around like this. We need to make a move, it's taking too long."

"You said you wanted to make sure you got them out together," Griff reminds me.

"I know I did but if there's a chance that Neve could be there tonight, then we need to go to wherever that location is."

"The docks, he's been asked to be at Purfleet Docks at Ten O' Clock."

I check my watch. It's almost nine now and I needed time to gather some men. "Already on it," grins Griff, reading my mind. "You go and kiss that kid of yours and meet me out front."

I find Sassy sitting where I'd vacated, and Alfie nowhere to be seen. She smiles, "I put him to bed. It was way past his bedtime. Can we talk?" She stands and I glance at the door where I know Griff is waiting.

"Actually, Sass I need to go. We've got a lead and Griff's waiting."

"A lead about Neve?" she asks, and I nod. "Well then I really need to say this before you go. I miss you Ryder. I didn't realise how much until you came back. When I saw you with Alfie, I knew we had to give us another go, for his sake. Before all that business with Alice we were great," she says, rushing her words out quickly.

I swallow hard, she's caught me off guard. I'd have given anything to hear those words all those years ago when I'd received my prison sentence. I used to lie awake at night racked with guilt about how I'd ripped my own family apart. "Say something, Ethan," she whispers, placing a hand on my chest. "We could have the perfect life, just the three of us. Don't we deserve that happiness?" My mind races, and I picture Sassy and Neve. They don't compare, Neve is my future. Before I can answer, she reaches up on her tip-toes and kisses me. Her sweet-smelling perfume fills my senses, her soft lips parting just enough to swipe her tongue against my mouth, forcing entry and taking full advantage of my stunned silence. Her arms trail around my neck and she presses herself against me, moaning softly into my mouth.

"What the fuck, Ryder!" Griff's voice startles me and I immediately step back, breaking all contact with her. "You're like the black fucking widow, Sassy, waiting to pounce. You made your choice when you banned me seeing my own damn nephew. You told me you were too good for this MC and you'd rather die than be back here and yet here you are trying to lure my brother back to you."

"I was upset, I caught my sister with my man. That's in the past. I want a family for Alfie." She turns to me, "I love you, Ryder, I always have."

I rub the back of my neck, my heart twisting painfully at the thought of Neve. This all feels wrong and I turn away, "I have to go," I mutter, heading for the exit.

Chapter Nineteen

Neve

"Wash," orders Finn angrily. He drops a bar of soap on the mattress where I lay. He'd had two buckets of warm water brought down to the cellar, and the other two girls had eagerly washed, happy to feel clean again.

"No," I mutter, turning my back to him and curling my knees up to my chest. I was still wearing the tatters of silver dress he'd ripped from me and I had no intention of stripping off in front of him.

"Fine," he mutters, moving away. I gasp when cold water hits me, sitting up and spluttering. "We'll do this my way." He then whistles and two men come down the steps. I watch in horror as they each position themselves beside the mattress. "Hold her," says Finn.

I scream in anger as they each grab a limb, pinning me to the bed. "Get off me," I yell, trying to fight them off.

"You always have to be so fucking stubborn," snaps Finn, picking up the bar of soap and rubbing it onto a sponge, "I asked you nicely." He shreds the remains of my dress and begins to wash me. I don't stop fighting, screaming at the top of my lungs until my throat aches in protest.

When he's finished and is satisfied that I'm clean, he grabs a bucket of water and swills me. The two men release me and leave. Finn throws a towel my way. "Dry off and then dress in that," he instructs, pointing to a dress sitting on the bottom step. "If you mess me around, I'll call those men back and I'm sure they'll come up with creative ways to make you comply."

"What's happening, Finn? Where are you going to take me. What did that man want and where's Harlee."

He spins back to me, pointing a finger in my face. "Fuck you, Neve. I don't owe you an explanation, not after what you did to me."

"Quit your bitching, you're still, here aren't you?" I yell angrily.

Finn shoves his hands in his pockets heads for the steps. "I told Ryder that he owed me a woman, what do you think I meant by that Neve?" He stops turning to face me again. "Alice was mine. We were meant to be, and he ruined everything. She died in his fucking arms," he hisses, balling his fists.

Everything suddenly makes sense. "It was you," I gasp, "You were the other man. You pushed her."

"Clever girl. It was all because of him. So now I'm taking you. I want him to suffer, to know what it feels like to lose the one person that you love more than anything. I was changing for her, I was going to be a better man."

"He went to prison for something he didn't do," I yell. "He's suffered enough. Fuck," I snap, "I bet it galled you when you knew we were together. You killed her, not him."

"It was an accident and he caused it. Now he's determined to make my life hell, stealing my shipments, taking my clients, offering my girls work at his strip club. He brought this on himself, so when you get to your new home with your new owner, think back to this and remember that he put you in this situation, he should have left me well alone."

"Finn, listen to what you're saying. I am the mother of your child, are you really going to use me to prove a point to Ryder? What about Harlee?"

"Harlee is fine. She'll be happy with Mary."

I bend slightly, the pain in my chest intensifying. "No Finn, no. Please, please don't take her away from me. You loved me once, how can you do this?"

"I loved you and then you ruined it by having her. You should have kept things the way they were."

"Think about Alice, would she want this? She wanted you to be better."

He marches over to me and I scramble back until I hit the wall. I screw my eyes closed, waiting for the blow but it doesn't come. "Don't ever speak about her again," he hisses, close to my face. "Now get dressed, we have to leave in five minutes." I watch as he leaves, and then the women rush over, wrapping me in their arms.

"Oh Neve," Adelina says with a sigh, "Poor Neve."

"I'm fine," I whisper, my words barely a whisper. "We have to be brave now. When we get a chance, we must run because they are going to sell us tonight to bad men. We can't let them sell us." Both women nod, stepping back so that I can pull on the short black dress. "If you get the chance to go on your own, then you must take it, don't stop to help me or they will kill you. Just run, fast."

Adelina repeated the same to Malia who nodded, with tears in her eyes.

The door opens again and Finn stands at the top. "Let's go," he snaps.

We all take each other's hands and I lead us up the steps. We have no shoes or underwear, just the short black dress and as we follow him out onto the gravel driveway, I wince as sharp stones stick to my feet.

We're instructed to get into a black Range Rover. Finn climbs in the front along with the driver. "The doors are child locked so don't get any ideas."

Ryder

I blow my warm breath into my hands. We've not long arrived but it's cold with a strong wind blowing off the Thames. Griff hands me a hat and I pull it on, grateful for extra warmth.

The place is dead, and although we're opposite the entrance to the docks, I'm still stressed thinking we might miss them. We've stationed thirty other men in and around the stacked shipping containers. All armed and all just waiting for my order.

I still when my earpiece crackles and Bear announces, "Three Vehicles approaching."

Two minutes later, three Vehicles turn into the docks and take a right, slowly driving in convoy. We wait until they're out of sight before Griff taps my shoulder and indicates for me to follow him. We weave in and out of containers as silently as we can until we spot the taillights on the third car, slowing down.

Crouching down behind a barrel, we wait as the vehicle doors open. Two security men in dark clothing step out first and open the doors on a container. They go back to the vehicle and drag a female from the back. She's struggling and fighting against them. I go to rush over but Griff stops me, shaking his head. "Wait," he whispers.

The guard slaps the girl hard and she screams. He holds her arms behind her back, "Gag the stupid bitch," he growls, and the other guard steps forward and proceeds to wrap material around the girl's face.

A second girl steps from the vehicle, dressed the same as the first, neither looked familiar. It's only when a third gets out that I gasp. Neve. Griff grabs my arm, smiling with relief. The doors to the other vehicles are opened and security wait with big umbrellas, keeping the men that get out, dry.

Neve

I see my opportunity. Adelina is being difficult, fighting against the man holding her. The other security men step in to help, leaving me and Malia to follow on. I squeeze Malia's hand and use my eyes to indicate that she should get ready. I glance back, Finn is shaking hands with other men, all smiling and greeting each other enthusiastically.

I give Malia's hand a small tug, before turning to run. Shouting rings out all around us, and I feel a hand brush against me, letting me know that there's someone hot on our tales. I daren't look back, instead I focus ahead. And then I lose my footing, the mud beneath me making it impossible to stay upright and I crash to the floor with Malia landing on top of me. Laughter comes from behind and humiliation burns me. We were so close.

Finn looms over me, laughing hard. And then he crouches, grabbing a handful of my hair and pulling me to my knees. "You stupid cunt," he hisses.

The click of a gun surprises us both and for a second, I think I'm hallucinating. "Get your hands off my old lady," growls Ryder, his voice low and menacing. I almost laugh with relief. I never thought I'd see him again after tonight.

Finn yanks me to him, standing with an arm around my waist. I feel something sharp pressed to my neck. "Good evening, Ryder. How nice of you to join us uninvited."

"I wouldn't do anything stupid if I was you, Finn, look around." My eyes trail over the men that appear from the shadows, all dressed in black, all armed. Finn is outnumbered, but he presses the blade harder into my skin and I begin to feel panic. He only wants Ryder to feel pain, and seeing my throat cut, would give him the best results.

"You're making a huge mistake, Ryder."

"Bigger than letting you live when I had the perfect opportunity to kill you?" asks Ryder. "I should have chased you down instead of comforting Alice. I should have slit your damn throat."

"Do you know what she told me, what she said before I pushed her?" Finn taunts. Ryder remains quiet and Finn laughs. "She told me she was pregnant with your fucking kid, pregnant by a scumbag."

Ryder remains calm but I can tell by the tick of his jaw this is new information to him. Finn continues, "She came to tell me it was over, she was leaving me because you and her were out in the open. Stupid bitch. There was no way I was letting her leave me for you, and then, even after all of that, you go after my wife. You must like my cast offs."

Ryder glares hard. "So then you let me take the blame for her death, even though it was you all along."

"Boo fucking who. You couldn't just leave it could you. You had to come and try and ruin me. Well fuck you. Have this stupid whore, she's useless to me anyway." He shoves me towards Ryder who catches me, sagging in relief as he grips me to him.

Suddenly, the place is bathed in blue. Police cars surround us. "Armed Police. Drop your weapons," shouts an officer.

I cling to Ryder harder, pushing my face into his chest. "Baby," he whispers, letting go of me. "We have to step apart, they aren't fucking about."

"No," I murmur, refusing to move.

"They have guns, Neve. Let me go. You're safe now."

A female officer gently take my arm. "Come with me," she whispers.

Ryder

Officers begin to cuff men. The chief of police comes over and Griff hands over the recording device. "Well done," he says, patting him on the back. "I'll be in touch."

"I'm sure you will," Griff utters. He hadn't been keen on making a deal, or even approaching the chief, but we had no choice. It was taking too long to get to Neve and this was the perfect opportunity to get Finn for what he did to Alice. Apparently, the chief had been playing Finn all along. The dinners and golf had all been a ploy to find out more about the shady shit he was doing. We decided to partner and nail the bastard. Plus the chief agreed to help us secure custody of Harlee and get an injunction against Finn, which means safety for my old lady.

"Where's Neve?" I ask and the chief points to a nearby police car.

"Ryder, you need to know that we found the house where Neve was kept. Harlee wasn't there." I give a nod, I'd suspected as much.

I go over to the car and the second Neve sees me, she climbs out, releasing the hands of the other two girls who are sobbing in relief.

"Have they got Harlee?" she asks.

I shake my head and she pales. "They're working on it Siren. We'll get her back."

"His house maid took her. Her name is Mary. She lost her own child. She looked after Finn when he was a kid."

"Okay baby, okay. I'll tell the chief. We'll get her back I promise."

Chapter Twenty

Neve

The mud caked to my skin is now dry, pulling it tight. As I climb from the car and stare up at the clubhouse, Ryder wraps his kutte around me. I glance at Griff as he leads Malia and Adelina into the club. "You're safe now," says Ryder, kissing her on the head.

"What will happen to the other two?" I ask.

He shrugs, "The chief wasn't happy about us bringing them back here, they're here illegally," he says. "But I hope we can swing a deal to help them." He places a hand at the small of my back and we go inside. "Go and shower, I'll make you a hot drink."

I get to the top of the stairs, loving the feel of carpet under my toes. I glance at the room where Harlee had slept and gently push the door. Surprised when I see Sassy curled up asleep on the bed, with Alfie. Tears fill my eyes and I feel Ryder rush up behind me, like he's suddenly remembered his ex was here.

"Siren, it isn't what it looks like," he mutters.

"It's fine," I whisper, swiping at my tears. "I just needed to smell her pillow," I add, almost laughing at how ridiculous that sounds out loud. "but it's fine." I rush to his bedroom.

I stand before the mirror and take in my swollen face, my black eyes and the bruises littering my skin. Then I lift the dress and stare in horror at the sight of more bruising and my sunken ribs.

Ryder stops in the doorway, his eyes staring wide as he takes in the scene. "Fuck."

I rush to try and cover up feeling ashamed and embarrassed but he moves quickly, taking my hands. "Don't," he growls, "You're beautiful. You'll always be beautiful to me no matter what, so please don't hide form me."

"I'm a mess," I sob. "And why the fuck is Sassy in Harlee's bed?"

"I don't know," he sighs.

"Did she jump in your bed too?" I snap, all my pain and danger surfacing.

"No Neve don't be ridiculous," he says with a sigh.

"Why is she here then?" I scream. "Why are they in my daughter's bed?" I begin to sob harder and he reaches for me, with sympathy on his face.

"Please baby, don't do this. You're tired. You need rest. I'll explain everything and answer all your questions tomorrow. Go and wash so we can sleep."

"How can I sleep, without Harlee? It's impossible. What if Mary took her far away? I don't know when she took her, they could have left the country. I haven't seen her for days."

"I don't know, Neve. I don't know where she is or what she's playing at taking someone else's daughter or even being a part of Finn's fucked up world. But without rest you'll be no good to Harlee when she comes home." He leads me to his bathroom and turns on the shower. "I'm going to make you that drink."

Ryder

I head back to where Sassy is sleeping and shake her awake. She smiles sleepily. "Hey."

"What the fuck are you doing here, Sarah?" I hiss.

She sits up, looking confused. "I told you I'd put Alfie to bed, I wasn't going to wake him."

"You put him in Harlee's bed," I snap.

"Oh, I'm sorry, I thought your son would be priority over your girlfriends kid," she snaps.

"I want you gone first thing. Harlee is missing and Neve came in here to see you in her daughters' bed. I'll be in touch about Alfie and if you start fucking me about with contact then I'll take you to court. He's my kid and I deserve the chance to get to know him away from you." I storm out and head down to the kitchen.

When I return to the bedroom with a mug of hot chocolate, I find Neve laying on the bed in one of my shirts. I smile, committing the image to memory. I've missed her so much.

"Were you hurt bad?" she asks sleepily. "I was worried you were dead."

"I was in hospital for a few days. Bleed on the brain apparently."

"When you didn't come for me, I assumed the worst."

I slide into bed behind her, not bothering to remove my damp clothes from the rain. I pull her to be, resting her head on my chest. "Siren, we've been trying to find you. Griff's spent hours making calls and plans to get you back to us. It was like you'd vanished. I couldn't think straight without you and so Griff really took the lead." I can't help feeling guilty for that.

"I knew you'd find me eventually," she whispers. "He took me to a big house. It was just out of London, I think. He had guards with guns and dogs patrolling. He wasn't like the Finn I knew."

I'm relieved she's talking about it. I haven't wanted to probe too much but I'm also desperate to know everything. "Did he lock you away?"

"Not at first. I think he was convincing us both we could work and showing off his house was part of that. But then I stole his mobile and he caught me. After that, he kept me locked in the cellar." She begins to cry again, "I didn't see Harlee after that."

"I was dead set on ending him tonight, Siren. I want the fucker dead. But Griff made me see sense. If he's dead, he can't tell us where Harlee is and she's my priority now. I have men out looking for them right now. I swear I won't give up."

"You can't go down for murder, Ryder. I need you here." She closes her eyes and I hold her until she's drifted off to sleep.

Neve

"Neve, wake up." I open my eyes to find Ryder shaking me gently. "Griff's tracked Mary."

I don't ask any questions, I shoot up out of bed and begin to pull on my clothes. Ryder rounds my side of the bed and takes my upper arms, halting me, "I think you should stay here, Siren," he says gently. "If Harlee isn't with her, it's another setback. And if she does have her, well that could end badly for Mary."

"If she is with her, she'll want me, Ryder. I can handle whatever comes. But I'm coming with you." He's crazy if he thinks I'm waiting here for news, even if Harlee isn't with her, she'll know where she is and I can appeal to her better nature, I'm sure of it.

It takes us an hour to get to the derelict looking house. There's not a soul around. No passing cars, no neighbours, not even a dog walker.

"Are you sure this is the right place?" Ryder asks Griff.

Griff nods, looking down at his iPad. "Her mobile was used at six this morning. It pinged up at this address."

"Let's go take a look then," I say, eagerly.

We get out of the car and cross the road. Ryder pushes on the small mental gate and it creaks as the rusty hinges rub together. Before we've even gone down the path, the front door swings open. Ryder pulls a gun from the back of his jeans, taking me by surprise. He drags me behind him as Mary steps from the property with her head down. She's rummaging through her bag paying no attention. "You need to stop there," growls Ryder and she looks up in surprise. Her wide eyes take in the scene before her and a whimper leaves her throat. "Oh Jesus," she whispers, dropping her bag and raising her hands. The contents spill across the floor and I can't help but scan them for any signs she's holding my little girl. A toy or a snack. Anything to give me hope.

"Where's Harlee?" I demand, pushing around Ryder so she can see me.

"Neve," she gasps.

"I want my little girl, Mary," I say, my tone desperate. "Where is she?" She doesn't answer quick enough and I begin to shout Harlee's name frantically.

Mary waves her hands, "Stop yelling," she hisses, "She's napping. She's absolutely fine, Neve."

My heart slams wildly in my chest and I run forward, ignoring Ryder who tries to grab hold of me. I shove Mary out of the way and run through the house, checking room to room until I finally spot my little girl curled up on the couch, fast asleep and unaware of the chaos spiralling around her.

I drop to my knees and run my hand over her hair, moving my nose into the crook of her warm neck and inhaling deeply. "Baby girl," I whisper. "I love you so much."

"Mummy?" She twists to face me and a sob escapes me as I pull back and smile down at her.

"Hey, Popple. How yah doing?"

"mummy, you're here," Harlee cries, wrapping her arms around my neck and clinging to me.

"I missed you so damn much," I whisper, holding her close.

"Is daddy gone?" she asks and I detect the worry in her voice.

"Daddy is gone forever, Popple. He will never come near us again."

Ryder

I step into the room to see my two favourite girls wrapped around each other. It warms my cold heart. "How are my ladies?" I ask and they pull apart slightly.

Harlee screams in delight, jumping from the couch and running to me. It almost brings a tear to my eye as I sweep her into my arms and her little arms cling to me. Neve saunters over and I open my arm, tucking her into my side and kissing her on the head. "Finn lied to Mary," I whisper. "Told her you had," I glance at Harlee who is still snuggled against me before whispering to Neve, "Dead."

"I just can't help wonder if she saw an opportunity," she mutters. "Finn made it sound like she was looking for a replacement for her own child."

"She seems genuinely pleased you're okay," I tell her.

"Mary promised to look after me until you could find us again," says Harlee, running her fingers into Neve's hair.

Neve nods, kissing Harlee on the cheek. "I need to go and speak to her for myself."

I give a nod and follow her outside. Mary is sitting on a bench in the front garden. "We need to talk," Neve says, coldly.

"I promised I'd look after her for you, Neve. I would never have hurt her."

I pass Harlee to Griff and she squeals excitedly as he whisks her away. Neve takes a seat beside Mary.

"What happened?" I demand.

"Finn started acting weird. Some deals went bad, the Italians pulled out leaving him stuck with two containers of guns and drugs that he couldn't shift. The Chief of Police was on his back about license agreements in two of his clubs. I think he felt like everything was going bad. He was acting erratic. I was worried for Harlee and so I just took her. Finn was talking like you were dead and the thought of Harlee knowing that, killed me, so I ran with her. I don't think Finn even noticed we were gone but I kept us moving just to be sure."

"What was your plan?" snaps Neve. "Keep Harlee forever?"

"No, of course not. I have been checking the news every day, waiting for news that you'd been found or that Finn was dead. I would never have stopped looking for you."

Neve scoffs. "You sat back while he did what he did. You're as much a part of it as he was."

"What was I supposed to do? Nobody that works for Finn walks away alive. If you leave, he finds you and kills you. If you stay, you're a part of it all. He'll come for me, eventually, my days are numbered."

"He's locked up," says Neve.

"He has friends in high places," says Mary. "He'll have time to think over everyone he thinks wronged him. I'll never be safe again."

Neve glances at me before saying, "Then come with us."

"Neve," I hiss.

"She can't stay here and wait for Finn to come after her. She doesn't deserve that. She kept Harlee safe. I owe her."

"You don't owe me anything, Neve," says Mary, patting her leg. "I'm so happy you're both safe now. Go and live your life now and take care of that little angel."

"You're coming with us!" says Neve, firmly. "I can't live my life knowing you're living in fear of him, just like I have for all these years."

"Neve," I mutter, shaking my head. "You don't even know this woman. She's spent years working for Finn."

Griff is heading back up the path. "I couldn't help but overhear," he says, looking annoyed. "And the pres is right, Neve."

"You said you needed help around the club," snaps Neve. "You haven't had a home cooked meal in forever. Mary can take care of the men."

"No," I snap. "Absolutely not."

"He's right," says Mary, gently. "I'll be fine, Neve. Honest."

"Mary, you're coming to live with us at the club," says Neve, standing. I glance at Griff who shrugs helplessly.

"Mary are you coming too?" cries Harlee excitedly.

"Fuck sake," I mutter, rubbing at my forehead in annoyance. I point at Mary, "I'm running checks. Anything comes up that I don't like and the deal is off."

Mary smiles. "Of course."

Chapter Twenty-One

Neve

I wince as the needle drags across my skin. I hate needles. It's taken Ryder two whole weeks of begging, pleading and bargaining to get me in this chair. And even after all his promises, I still needed two shots of tequila and a double whiskey. We'd even argued over my tattoo placement. I wanted it somewhere more discreet, like my hip but Ryder had refused point blank hating the thought of another man touching me there. So now, as I stare at the ink seeping into my wrist, with Ryder holding my other hand, I smile. He was right, it does look good having his name on me.

He didn't even hesitate to have my name in large, scrolled letters over his heart. And then he got Harlee to write her name right underneath, alongside Alfies, which he then had tattooed. We're on his skin forever and that feels special. For the first time in months, years even, I feel relaxed and happy.

There is no threat of Finn turning up and causing me problems, or worse, him taking custody of our little girl. My new restraining order covers us both and lasts until Harlee turns eighteen, by which time, we're able to re-apply should we need it. But if Ryder is right, he's going away for a very long time.

And since our return to the club, Ryder has been amazing. He's been patient and understanding, and hardly left my side. I'm thankful for that because being around him makes me feel safer than I've ever felt. I close my eyes and think back to last week when he confessed to his kiss with Sassy. Don't get me wrong, I thought for a spilt second, things were over and I hated that feeling.

"Baby, I have to tell you something, it's eating me up inside and before I make us official, I have to clear it with you." Ryder took both my hands in his, which alarmed me because he looked so serious and worried.

"If this is gonna upset me, Ryder, its best you don't tell me. I'm a woman on the edge after everything that's happened."

"If I don't tell you, we're starting off all wrong and I don't want that for us, Siren. Just remember, I love you so much and you're my world. And please let me explain before you go bat-shit." My heart hammers, I know this isn't going to be good. I've never seen Ryder look so uncertain. "Sassy kissed me when you were held by Finn." He paused, letting his words sink in which is his first mistake because he doesn't see my slap coming. It takes him off guard and he clutches his cheek. "Fuck, woman, that hurt."

"You swore you two were done, Ryder. How the fuck did she kiss you?"

"We are done. She caught me by surprise, landing one on me when I was feeling vulnerable."

I scoff. "How was she even close enough to kiss you?"

"Baby, it was a misunderstanding. She'd seen me vulnerable the night before and she was worried. She woke up with strange ideas about us getting back together, but I put her straight. I love you, end of."

I'd pause in my manic pacing at his words and I can tell by his face he instantly regrets them in the way he winces. "Woke up?" *I repeat.* "She woke up where exactly?"

"Okay baby, before you fly off the handle let me explain. I got drunk, like so drunk I passed out. I woke and she was..."

Rage courses through me. "Do not tell me she was in your bed, Ryder, do not say those words."

"We were fully clothed, I had no idea she was even there. Nothing happened, I promise." *I try to leave the room, needing distance between us but he blocks my path.* "Neve, you promised to let me finish"

"I am so mad, like crazy mad," *I hiss, clenching my fists.*

"I love you. Nothing is going on with me and Sassy. I put her straight and told her that from now on she needed to stay the hell away from me. I want to see Alfie away from her. She agreed, she apologised-"

"She did not apologise to me. She sat in her fucking office talking to me about Harlee's trauma," *I yell.* "Neither of you said a word."

"Look, she's due any second to drop Alfie off, please calm down. I swear it was one time and a massive mistake. I love you. I told her that and she accepted it. Don't let this come between us, Siren, I'm begging you."

"How would you feel?" *I ask, arching a brow.* "If I'd kissed another man, an ex, even. Finn for example?"

He doesn't like the image I just put in his head and his fists clench at his sides. "I'd understand that you love me," *he grits out through clenched teeth.*

"Bullshit," *I yell.*

"Okay," *he snaps,* "I'd rip his fucking head off. But I wouldn't love you any less, baby. You're my everything. My world. You and Harlee are my future."

"And she knows that, does she?" Sassy enters the club and Ryder groans. "You really should have timed it better, babe," I spit, pushing past him and heading directly for Sassy.

She looks surprised as I march up to her. She releases Alfie's hand and he rushes off to find Harlee. "Do you have something you need to say to me?" I snap.

Her eyes glance past me, probably to Ryder. "Did I miss something?" she asks innocently.

"Yeah you missed the part where you stupidly tried it on with my old man thinking that shit was okay. Well let me tell you something, you stuck up bitch. I am his ol' lady now and I won't let that shit slide. You keep your manicured witchy fingers to yourself and we'll get along just fine."

I feel Ryder behind me and he places his hand on my lower back, letting her know we're a team. She nods stiffly. "Understood."

I turn to Ryder, reaching up and placing a kiss to his lips. "You let another bitch kiss these lips again and I won't be so understanding, do you hear me, Ryder?"

His eyes blazed with heat and he tugged me in for a deeper kiss. "Understood, Siren."

The tattoo gun switches off and I blink away the memories. Ryder smiles proudly at his name on my skin. "Fuck, Siren, that shit is hot."

Ryder

I stare around at the packed-out club. Brothers have travelled far and wide to come here to celebrate me and my old lady.

Neve leans into me. "Everyone is so nice," she whispers. "Just thinking that all these people will be here for me and Harlee, blows my mind. We're so lucky."

"I'm the lucky one, Siren."

I'd offered to buy us a house, one where we could grow our family, but Neve was set on staying at the club full-time. She clearly loves this huge family of bikers and that makes me happy. It takes a special kind of woman to put up with us.

Mya rushes over and grab's Neve's wrist, "Let me see."

Neve proudly shows off my name and they hug. Mya hasn't quite forgiven me for refusing to let her in on all the shit that was happening when Neve got taken. It was club business, something she didn't understand. But having her and Harlee back seems to have thawed her ice heart a little towards me and she gives me a small smile.

Mary rushed past with a tray of food. "Do you need help?" asks Neve but Mary shakes her head, smiling wide when a few bikers help themselves to her food. She seems to have settled well, and she adores feeding us, taking so much pride in everything she does. And although I haven't voiced it out loud, she's been worth her weight in gold around here, keeping the place spotless and making sure there's a home cooked meal on the table every evening.

Everything seemed to be slotting into place. Finn was facing life inside, Neve was back with me and settled. Harlee was back in school and loving her counselling sessions to help her understand what had happened. And he was having weekly visits with Alfie.

I place a kiss on Neve's head, "Yah know, all we need now is a baby and we're complete."

She smirks. "I think you've already started working on that plan, don't you?"

We haven't used protection at all since her return but neither of us have brought it up. "A Christmas baby would be nice."

She laughs, "Um, Christmas is exactly nine months away, what are the chances."

I slap her backside, pulling her closer, "We better get to work now."

Epilogue

Neve

"Ryder please will you just calm the hell down," I hiss, rubbing my hand over my swollen stomach. "My bag is by the door. All you need to do is get the damn bag and call the hospital to let them know we are on the way."

"You're still in the bath, Neve," snaps Ryder, his eyes wide in alarm.

"It helps with the pain, Mary suggested it."

"Is Mary a nurse, is she a midwife? I think we just need to go. What if it pops out in the bath?" His voice comes out high pitched in panic and I laugh.

"Deep breaths, Ryder, take nice deep breaths." Another contraction rumbles across my abdomen and I grab the edge of the tub, "Fuuuuck," I groan.

Ryder crouches beside the bath, watching me closely. "That's it, baby, breath, pant through it."

"You pant at the end, when you're pushing. You'd know that if you'd have been to more than one birthing class," I hiss. We'd argued more than once about the issue. Ryder had attended the first class and refused to come to anymore because he hated how everyone looked at him. He's right, they did, but as I pointed out, he's a big ass biker covered in tattoos, it's hard to picture him as the big softy I know he is. In the end I had to resort to taking Griff with me just so I wasn't alone. Ryder had made his brother relay every detail after each session.

"Get Griff," I bark, breathing through another contraction. They were definitely getting closer together.

"Griff is not coming in here whilst you're naked!"

"Ryder, your brother is gay, he doesn't find any of this attractive. And besides, he was my birthing partner in those classes that you refused to go to."

"I'll get him when you're fully clothed and not before."

I laugh at his jealousy. Secretly, I love how possessive he is over me.

I wait for the contraction to finish and push to my feet. Ryder grabs a towel and helps dry me off. We go into the bedroom and I pull on one of his t-shirts and a pair of knickers. He eyes me and I arch a brow, daring him to say anything. He presses his lips into a fine line.

"You realise the knickers will come off in the labour suite, right? Like I can't get this baby out without people looking down there."

He groans, "Let's not talk about that."

"Ryder, seriously, you need to stop. The doctor might be a male and he's going to look inside my vagina." He covers my mouth playfully and I laugh hard. "He's going to see it all," I continue.

Ryder slams his lips to mine, shutting me up as he swipes his tongue into my mouth. When he's certain I won't tease him anymore, he pulls back. "I love you."

"I love you too, now go and find my birthing partner."

Ryder

I'm a panicking mess. I can't help it. No amount of Griff telling me to stay calm, is working. Knowing Neve's in pain, rips me apart.

We each take an arm and help her into the hospital where a nurse rushes over with a wheelchair and whisks us into a room. The lighting is low and there's calming music playing in the background. It's nothing like I imagined it to be.

We get Neve onto the bed and the nurse smiles, "We need to remove the underwear, Neve so we can examine you."

Griff goes to hook his fingers into my old lady's knickers and I almost combust. He laughs as I slap his hand away. The nurse hands me a sheet to cover over Neve's lower half and then I remove her underwear, glaring at Griff the entire time.

The midwife lifts the sheet slightly and goes about her examination. After a few seconds she smiles, "Well, Neve, looks like you've done some great work all by yourself, you're nine centimetres. This baby is coming soon."

"Thank fuck," pants Neve.

The midwife gives her some gas and air. "Do you know what you're having?"

"I think a girl, he thinks a boy," says Griff.

"I'll go and update my colleagues, and we'll be back to find out!"

Once she's left Griff laughs hard, "She totally thinks we're a couple," he says. "She thinks Neve is our rent-a-womb."

Neve sucks harder on the gas and I glare at my brother. "Fuck no, Griff, that shit ain't funny. Stop playing up to it."

When the nurse returns, it was with two other midwifes. All females, much to my delight. "Who do we have here then?" asks one of them.

Neve takes the plastic tube from her mouth, "The father, the uncle, the mother," she mumbles.

"I'm the father," I say, firmly, "He is the uncle, my brother, nothing to do with the baby apart from being the uncle."

Griff laughs again. "Relax Ryder, they know just by looking at you, that you're too butch and manly to be gay," he says, before turning to the women and adding, "He just wanted to make it clear that he's straight."

Neve begins to moan, it's low and deep. "I need to push," she grunts.

"Go ahead," says the midwife, slightly lifting the sheet to look. "Let your body tell you what to do, Neve."

"You stay up this end," I warn Griff who salutes while smirking.

"Both of you stay this end," Neve snaps, grabbing me by the shirt and hauling my face close to hers. She then begins to growl, tucking her chin to her chest and squeezing her eyes closed.

"That's it, Neve, I can see the head," the midwife says with a grin. "You're doing amazing."

"Fuccccckkkkkkk," she screams, releasing my shirt and grabbing my hand instead.

"The head's out," the midwife informs us.

"That was quick work, Siren," says Griff, glancing at Neve's parted legs.

"Eyes," I snap, "Eyes up here."

"Chill Ryder, I don't want to look at your wife's butchered vagina," he smirks.

"My vagina is not butchered," Neve hisses, sucking heavily on the gas.

"One more push and this baby will be out," says the midwife.

Neve pushes, squeezing my hand so tight, I feel like it's breaking. Suddenly, a baby's cry fills the room and my eyes widen. I watch as she lifts a screaming bundle, placing it on Neve's chest. "Congratulations, you have a baby boy," she announces. "And," she adds, looking at her watch, "It's the first baby of the year for this hospital, it's twelve-o-nine in the morning."

I press my lips to Neve's head, staring at my gorgeous baby boy nuzzling into her chest. "Congrats, man," says Griff, slapping my on the shoulder.

I watch as Neve lifts her top, feeding our son right away. The midwife smiles, "You're a pro at this," she says.

"You're a fucking warrior," I whisper into her hair. "I'm in awe of you."

"Have you got a name?" asks the midwife.

Neve sighs heavily, "I told these clowns they could pick it if we had a boy."

I exchange a smirk with Griff who says, "Caidence."

"Really?" asks Neve, screwing up her face, "You want to call him Caidence, this precious tiny baby, it sounds like a dog's name."

"You said we could choose," shrugs Griff.

"Caidence," she repeats, looking down at her baby boy. "Sorry Caid, I should have thought it through better, but on the plus side, no one will bully you because you have loads of big uncles to protect you."

"This kid will kick arse, he won't need protection."

Caid finishes feeding and Neve holds him up for me to take. I shrug from my kutte and rip of my shirt, taking my boy and placing him against my chest. Neve smirks, "Man, if I hadn't have just given birth."

I snigger, kissing her on the lips. "Baby, we're gonna work on baby number two the second you're up to it."

"Four kids?" she says arching a brow.

"We gonna need a whole football team just so I can watch you boss that shit all over again. You're fucking amazing, mama, I love you so much.

She smiles, letting her eyes drift closed. "I love you two, Ryder. Happy New Year."

THE END

Social Media

[My Facebook Page](#)
[My Facebook Readers Group](#)
[Bookbub](#)
[Instagram](#)
[Goodreads](#)
[Amazon](#)
I'm also on

About the Author

Nicola Jane, a native of Nottinghamshire, England, has always harboured a deep passion for literature. From her formative years, she found solace and excitement within the pages of books, often allowing her imagination to roam freely. As a teenager, she would weave her own narratives through short stories, a practice that ignited her creative spirit.

After a hiatus, Nicola returned to writing as a means to liberate the stories swirling within her mind. It wasn't until approximately five years ago that she summoned the courage to share her work with the world. Since then, Nicola has dedicated herself tirelessly to crafting poignant, drama-infused romance tales. Her stories are imbued with a sense of realism, tackling challenging themes with a deft touch.

Outside of her literary pursuits, Nicola finds joy in the company of her husband and two teenage children. They share moments of laughter and bonding that enrich her life beyond the realm of words.

Nicola Jane has many books from motorcycle romance to mafia romance, all can be found on Amazon and in Kindle Unlimited.

Printed in Great Britain
by Amazon